BLUE GARDENIA 

Blue Gardenia

Amanda Gilby

LITERARY KITCHEN

SANTA FE/PORTLAND

This is a work of fiction. Unless otherwise indicated, all the names, characters, places, events and incidents in this book are either the product of the author's imagination or used in a fictitious manner. Any resemblance to actual persons, living or dead, or actual events is purely coincidental.

Blue Gardenia
Copyright © 2025 Amanda Gilby

First edition published September 2025 Literary Kitchen
ISBN: 978-1-950272-43-3

Book design by Barış Şehri
https://sehribookdesign.com/
Edited by Ariel Gore

NANA WANDA
PAPA JOE
PAUL
DEENIE
MARK
SADIE
MIA
JESS
JAKE
SARAH
AMELIA

SPRING

1. JESS

After the last leaf fell from the tree outside of our bedroom window, his posture started to deteriorate. He left for work and returned home in the dark. We attempted conversation over dinner, but the children demanded his attention. I washed the dishes and fell asleep reading bedtime stories. After I stumbled back into our empty room in the middle of the night, I listened to his feet drag across the hardwood floors as he shuffled from his office to the kitchen to pour another drink. If Jake didn't come to bed by 2 a.m., he didn't intend to sleep. I wrapped myself in gray flannel and pulled the heavy quilt over my nose. The wind picked up and a slow moan from the chimney transformed quiet rain into icy drops tapping on the window. Tucking the quilt in around my edges, I recalled the way my hands and feet felt in the folds of his body. I took his warm limbs for granted.

Deenie came back to me that winter. Adrift in a king-sized bed, I closed my eyes and transported myself to springtime in the garden, craving the sun on my cheeks and the first inch of baked earth in between my fingers. Deenie lived in the garden and in Grandpa's memories. She lived in photographs like the black and white picture he took of her squinting in the relentless Arizona sunshine. Mischief traveled from her eyebrows to the curve of her laugh lines in a smile reserved for her lover behind the camera. In the bottom corner of the photo, a spellbound stranger watched her from the side. I imagined being the sort of woman who provoked that look from strangers—who would lean over the local bar reading Neruda one night and dance on top of it the next.

As a child, I sipped ginger ale through a cocktail straw at that same bar on weekday afternoons with Grandpa. After a couple of beers, he looked off to the side as if someone projected his memories onto the wall. He described Deenie's eyes the first time they met in a booth ten feet away from us, or the time she climbed out onto a ledge in a Utah canyon, or when she ran through the desert in a monsoon. Back then, my grandmother was my favorite ghost story and a mystery I meant to solve.

In Deenie's garden, Grandpa opened a door to an alternate plane of existence where she attended my childhood tea parties as an imaginary guest. I talked to her through the peonies and listened for her whispers in the tall grasses Mom and Aunt Sadie transplanted beyond the birch tree. Secretly hoping some of Deenie's magic might have been passed on to me, I worked beside them in the garden as they attempted to preserve something of their mother through the beauty she cultivated. Over time, Deenie faded alongside my other childhood fantasies. The spring and summer weekends spent tending her flowers became a chore to help my family, and Deenie became a relic of the past— irrelevant to a young person living for the future.

I found her again when the dreams that once propelled me fizzled into a singular dream that consumed me—motherhood. Life transitioned into long days that poured out into longer nights, with more time to think and fewer original thoughts than ever before. The old stories about Deenie became kindling for the warmth I craved that long, lonely winter—a flame in the darkness that might reveal a more interesting part of me buried beneath parenting books and self-doubt. Waiting for spring, I arranged and rearranged stories and impressions of a woman I never met. After the buds on the tree outside our bedroom window started to open, Jake slept beside me every night again, but my fascination with Deenie continued to grow.

The night air was hot for the end of April. The curtains drifted elegantly away from the open window revealing white blossoms on the Callery Pear tree. I welcomed the cool breeze but not the blooms' rancid semen stench. The city planted those trees to beautify our old Pittsburgh neighborhood, but the heavy odor terrorized anyone brave enough to walk outside in the spring. Sleep came in the easy, delicious way it does when accompanied by too much red wine after dinner, but the spell broke a few hours later. I startled awake with a deep, quick inhale. After several calming breaths, the palpitations eased. Hoping to fall back to sleep, I closed my eyes and tried to merge with the last image I recalled from a dream, but the residual adrenaline denied me.

Slowly opening my eyelids over tacky eyes, I turned toward Jake and matched my breathing to his. The familiar pattern and tone of his snoring were a comfort on those nights. When he took too long in between breaths, I put my hand on his chest and he responded with a happy, content sort of sigh. Too tired to move, too thirsty to lay there, I sat up and listened to his apneic snores, faint bass sounds from the rowhouse next door, and the train rumbling past the river down in The Flats. Mesmerized by the lovely and horrible white-blossomed limbs waving outside my window, my thoughts settled back to the unsolvable Deenie.

My mom and Aunt Sadie were children when they lost their mother, so Grandma Deenie existed in my mind as the woman in my mom's favorite picture. Grandpa often mentioned how much I resembled Deenie with the same dark, wavy hair and blue eyes. I conjured her image at the end of my bed: 1950's glamorous with glossy red lips and a self-tailored dress accentuating every curve. I pulled back a handful of my own coarse, dark frizz with a hair tie and reached down beside my bed for the t-shirt I peeled off earlier. Pulling it over my head, tent-like over those famous curves, my fingers brushed against a familiar crust at the bottom. My girls both had colds.

Mom loved to say that Grandma Deenie put more energy into her garden than her children. She rarely talked about her mother but alluded to Deenie's diary years ago. When I pressed her about it, she laughed.

"Who wants to read the ramblings of a crazy woman?" she said and changed the subject before I could answer.

She'd never say *crazy woman* around Aunt Sadie, who had a different take on the garden.

"Mama needed a place to put all those emotions," Aunt Sadie told me. "When she didn't know how to love us, she turned her love into flowers."

I didn't understand how Deenie's life and death must have affected my mom and Aunt Sadie. On one of the evenings that she chose the flowers over her daughters, she accidentally cut herself, working without gloves. They said the infection traveled into her blood, killing her within days.

Grandpa offered me Deenie's wedding band before I married Jake. He held it between our faces and placed it in my palm like holy communion. Looking down at the band on my finger, I imagined it on her hand: white gold spiraling diamond chips into delicate tulips on both ends. As I approached the age my grandmother was when she died, I could better trace the line from her hand to mine. Deenie didn't let motherhood define her. She felt like a door to a more vibrant place within me that might drive some fresh air into that stifling, sour spring.

Thirst eventually won out. I carefully stepped over our black dog lying beside the bed and avoided the creakiest floorboards on my way to the door. Before I reached the stairs, I followed the pull into my daughters' room on the opposite side of the hallway. Facing the back yard and sheltered from the sounds of the city, it smelled like freshly-turned soil and the promise of rain. Drawn toward their bed, I laid the palm of my hand on the rise and fall of my youngest daughter's strawberry print nightgown. After a few minutes, the floor across the hall creaked and Jake appeared in the doorway.

"What's the verdict, Jess? Still beating?" he asked with a wry smile.

Backlit by the street light peeking through from across the hall, he looked like a boy leaning against the doorway. He had a particular way of tilting his head that reminded me of the way we used to love each other before life got complicated.

"Still beating, still breathing...we've managed to keep them alive for another day."

"Good." With eyes closed, he pushed dirty blond hair away from his face.

He turned back toward our room, but his anxiety lingered in the air like humidity. He worried about my worrying. He didn't worry that the girls were still breathing in their beds, or how much they ate, or if he spent enough time with them. He went to his tedious office job every day so I could be home and wondered why I ever felt unhappy when I had everything I wanted.

After he left, my eyes went right back down to our girls. My oldest, Sarah, slept with her arms wrapped around her stuffed snowman and a dark swath of hair plastered to her face with drool. Seeing her that way, no one could guess what a force lived inside of that sleeping four-year-old. She spent her days turning things upside down to uncover some new wonder–smelling, tasting and touching everything in her path. She devoured each new experience with so much excitement that her words stumbled over each other, built up, collapsed and bubbled out of her mouth in explosions.

My baby Amelia slept next to her in a matching nightgown. I could barely see her fair skin and bow lips under the mess of blond curls. As an infant, she rarely cried. From my arms, she observed her surroundings with remarkable concentration. At nearly two and a half, Amelia walked one step behind her sister when she wasn't attached to me, with one hand down my shirt and the other in my hair.

"What is she so *afraid* of Jess?" My mom would ask, watching Amelia's hand fly down the front of my shirt. "She's holding on for dear life."

It wasn't fear; she watched and waited. When Amelia spotted something she wanted, she went for it. If I took my eyes off of her for longer than a few minutes, I might find her scaling a bookcase to get her hands on something that sparkled near the window or tempted her with velvet promises. My tactile baby brushed her discoveries over her rosy cheeks to decide if they were worth keeping.

I counted the minutes to get to the end of the day, but missed my girls when the house went quiet. In a room covered with glowing, plastic stars and littered with books and blocks and naked dolls, I watched them sleep and wondered, like Jake, why I ever felt unhappy when I had everything I wanted. It mystified my mom. She loved being a mother and grandmother. Since we lost my stepdad, Mark, she treasured those roles more than ever.

As children, Mom and Aunt Sadie sometimes went days without seeing their mother. Deenie emerged after they were tucked in for the night and my mom—little Mia, stayed awake to watch her work in the garden from the bedroom window. At the end of every night, Deenie cut flowers to leave by her daughter's beds—payment for nurturing owed.

As I sat in the dark searching for a reason to feel worthy of my sleeping daughters, I felt a new connection to Grandma Deenie. Why be grateful at the end of the day and not at the beginning? Deenie might've told me about the dark emotions of motherhood: the audacity of ever regretting your children, and yet, loving them fiercely in spite of it. The gravity of it all kept me awake and wishing I had something to occupy those nights like Deenie did. Her garden was hallowed ground, but it wasn't where she died; it's where she lived.

It was time to find Grandma Deenie's diary.

2. MIA

Mia, Mia, Mia, I tell myself—this path you're on is a *slippy* slope, talking to your dead husband. You'd correct my Pittsburghese there, wouldn't ya, Mark?

"Slippy isn't a word," you'd say, shaking your head.

I'm telling ya, honey, walking onto this porch is entering another dimension. You spent so much time out here toward the end; I think you opened something up with one foot in the world and one in the astral plane. On our old wooden swing, I watch the sky as the wind blows through the oak trees behind me. The branches sway the hollow, metal tubes of the giant wind chimes you hung the year before you got sick. They echo deep and resonant like a choir of monks and I feel myself becoming entranced—then, you appear.

Maybe this is *my* nervous breakdown and there's more of Mama in me than I'd like to admit. I know you're surprised to hear me talk about her. After I lost you, the grief that flooded through me unearthed things I didn't even remember burying and now I think about her all the time.

Nervous breakdown. Manic Depressive. The grown-ups grasped at terms they never used before to understand something they'd never encountered. Mama had a *nervous breakdown* in the fall of '64 when Mrs. Carini found her naked in the garden, soil rubbed into every pore. She called my father to run out and cover Mama with an old, rough blanket while I watched from the window of my childhood bedroom. Nana Wanda called it a nervous breakdown, but only in whispers to my father when they thought I wasn't listening. We knew Sadie inherited Mama's erratic nature, but maybe losing you finally broke me.

Whenever I wake up, or come home, my first instinct is still to find you. Your death hasn't changed that. I told my sister. Of course, Sadie thinks it's wonderful—communicating with the dead. She sent a postcard last week from Upstate New York—bright blue with *Lily Dale Assembly* in gold letters. *World's Largest Center for the Religion of Spiritualism* followed, with a picture of a floating white lily on a green pad.

> April 24, 2009
> Dear Mia, Lily Dale is peaceful-an excellent
> retreat. We should come back someday. The
> shaman I'm working with understands bipolar
> disorder. She's helping me to understand
> how to swim through, rather than drown. It's
> fascinating. (Yes, I'm taking my medication.)
> Her neighbor is a medium. I told her that you've
> been talking to Mark. Lots to discuss-home
> by Friday and looking forward to being with
> you and Jess in Mama's garden. Love, Sadie

She'll be roping me into a seance for a message from Mama. I do appreciate the postcards though. After everything that happened last August, she knows how I worry whenever she goes away. It's unheard of for a teacher to call off work the first week of school, but what choice did I have? I got the first flight out and brought her back home. Jess was so good about pitching in while Sadie rested and got her meds back on track. We've had our ups and downs with her illness, but that one left a mark on all of us. We could've lost her.

I figured she'd try to get out of the garden work this year, with Daddy gone and the house empty. She started wandering around the planet last winter, searching for new ways to heal: last month a meditation retreat and this month a shaman with a psychic neighbor. As if I'd talk about me and you to a stranger; I'd sound like a crazy person.

How would I explain it? After you died, I woke every morning feeling like the day before was a hazy dream I could barely remember. Days added up to weeks of faint recollections and fuzzy images of paperwork, visitors, and cards received and sent. I kept myself so busy that I didn't think to look for you, until I came home on an otherwise entirely normal day (if anything could be considered normal after your death) and went out to the front porch to find you looking out at the world. When I said your name, you turned around to look at me.

I'm not sure how Jess would take it, if she knew that we still talked. It makes me nervous. I know—what else is new? This anxiety isn't the usual bumpy edges, dips, and curves. It's more of a flat and endless road before and behind me, enticing my mind to wander and do crazy things, like talk to my dead husband.

Last night, I listened to this writer at the library talk about the parts of life that are too profound for words. I tried to imagine describing what you did for me. Before I met you, I didn't know how to identify the constellations or how many different kinds of moss existed. As a child, I spent years on the floor in the back of the library, paging through words that I didn't quite understand, but loved to read and say. When we met, you translated everything until it became mine, and now it can never *not* be mine.

Life before you was hot dogs and frozen pierogies boiled until all of the potato seeped out into the water, leaving an empty, rubbery shell. Unless we went to Nana's, where life was, in sporadic bursts, homemade chicken soup with thick egg noodles and butter pecan ice cream, and maybe, on Christmas eve, freshly made pierogies plump with mushrooms and cabbage, fried in butter with onions. You met me as a woman whose life was mostly hot dogs and walked with me as the world unfurled like a fern, into fresh figs with endive and king trumpet mushrooms.

There are so many birds out today. Look at that goldfinch in the dogwood. These trees are beautiful in the spring with their pink and white blossoms, but I'm ready for the leaves to come in. It's been a long winter and I miss the green. Green is closer to you. It's pulling off the main road and down the hill to the back of our house, under that canopy of leaves, feeling ten degrees cooler on a hot day. It's easier to breathe in green. You open your eyes—green, and tell me everything I need to know with your smile.

I ran into Donna and Bill the other day. Remember when we decided he had the face of a young Jerry Garcia? After that, we figured out that neither of us had ever listened to The Grateful Dead. You got a joint from Bill and brought it out here with iced tea and snacks while I braided my hair—long back then. We spent a whole afternoon, right after Jessie moved out, listening to *Europe '72*.

Deep into a ten-minute song, I could still feel tiny pockets of tension in my body, as if it anticipated a potential interruption from Jess. You laughed at me.

"Like a teenager afraid of getting caught," you said.

I'd never made a choice for myself without considering Jess. Little cords connected to every pocket of tension reached out from my body toward Jess or Sadie and pulled me away from that moment with you. I sunk into the chair and imagined the cords coming loose and floating away in the wind. You were on the hammock, like today, watching the sun melt into a hundred shades of pink and red and I watched you with gratitude vibrating in my bones. I can close my eyes and feel the same buzzing in my toes and fullness in my belly right now. After you died, I didn't think I'd ever feel it again, but here I am. Here we are.

I can't remember when I started feeling gratitude more than sadness. It must have been so gradual that I didn't realize it happened. Once you hear that perfect song, read that perfect line, eat fresh figs with endive—I guess there's no going back.

3. JESS

After a few hours of intermittent thunderstorms, a cool breeze blew in from across the hallway. I pulled the sheet over my shoulders and listened for a moment to the quiet house. 9 a.m. on the clock—Jake let me sleep in and took the girls out to make my escape easier. The smell of freshly-made coffee carried me downstairs where I found a chocolate chip muffin next to the pot. I recognized it from the market a few doors down, where Jake took the girls for donuts on Sundays.

Afraid to squander the gift of an easy exit, I ate quickly, dressed, and saved my second cup of coffee for the twenty minute drive west across the city to Presston. Resurrecting the garden with Mom and Sadie was a yearly ritual, but that particular morning felt significant. I hadn't been back to the house since Grandpa died and it would probably be our last year in the garden. When we lived in Presston, I spent countless afternoons in Grandpa's attic looking through photos, trying on hats, and dusting off old books. Deenie lived on in the garden, but the attic held the remnants of her life and hopefully her diary.

I drove for miles beside the river and followed it to the McKees Rocks Bottoms, which made up about two-thirds of a sort of peninsula jutting out into the river, with Presston accounting for the other third. Light gleamed from the gold domes of the Eastern Orthodox church. The smell of fried onions seeped into the closed windows of my car as I passed the homemade sign near the sidewalk: PYROHY TODAY 12 TO 4. Four breathtaking churches lined one short block in a historically humble neighborhood—the Eastern Orthodox church, the Ukrainian Catholic church, and two Roman Catholic churches. At the stop sign, my eyes followed the blue, cross-topped steeple pointing into the clear sky. Mom loved to retell stories about walking to St. Mary's with Nana Wanda—every Sunday and sometimes during the week for daily mass. The building that housed the bakery across the street sat empty that day. Mom's been trying to replicate their peanut butter cookies for years. Sipping my coffee, I drove under the bridge and passed the old *Hose House*, the Presston volunteer fire department with a full bar inside. Grandpa volunteered to drink with his buddies there on the days he didn't go to the beer garden.

A hawk flying over the rail yard caught my attention as I turned onto the industrial road. I grew up identifying Presston as my *town,* though it was nothing more than a pair of dead end streets, at the dead end of a long industrial road—one road to get in or out. As kids, a friend and I walked halfway down that road as the sun set. I'll never forget the terror of the light fading with neither end in sight. On the left side, I passed a mile of train cars sitting idle on the track near the road. The old factories stood behind fences and brick walls on the right side. Many of them were deserted, including the shuttered Pressed Steel Car Company.

The Pressed Steel Car Company built Presston: two streets lined with identical twin homes to house workers for the company or what Nana Wanda (Deenie's mom) called *the slaughterhouse.* Her husband, Papa Joe, lost two fingers working there. Nana Wanda helped raise my mom and Aunt Sadie after Deenie died, but I never knew her. Her parents left Poland and moved to Presston right after the big strike of 1909 when the company recruited mostly Eastern European immigrants to work in perilous conditions for a pittance. The Presston that birthed Nana Wanda had a suspicious nature, a legacy of suffering, and a streak of revolt.

The industrial road ended at the old footbridge that crossed over the rail yard to the far end of McKees Rocks. I turned right onto Ohio Street and passed the beer garden on the corner where Deenie met my Grandpa Paul in 1954. The two long, parallel streets of Presston were connected by a street in the middle creating a giant H. The rail yard and industrial road bordered the bottom of the H and one long set of railroad tracks traveled alongside the river at the top of the H. Beyond the town, the tracks from the bottom met up with the tracks by the river and chugged toward the sunset.

Halfway up the street, at the stop sign, I came to the edge of the community park, just ahead on my right. In the corner, near the colorful, spinning disc of the merry-go-round, a historical marker memorialized the *Bloody Sunday Uprising of 1909*. When I was old enough to read and understand it, I spent a summer obsessed with learning everything I could about that time. Grandpa had newspaper clippings from the anniversary, when they dedicated the memorial. The local coroner estimated that, on average, a Pressed Steel worker died every single day before the uprising.

Grandpa tried to explain. "Imagine they got ten dollars from the company, then eight dollars went to rent and five to the company store for food. Every week those poor folks owed more money to the company than they earned. It snowballed and they never got outta debt. All for a job risking life and limb? When the company started throwin' people outta their homes, they fought back."

After the strike and the months of violence that followed, the company made small, incremental concessions—a wage increase and a promise to end the abuses, but it would always be the slaughterhouse to Nana Wanda's generation.

By the time Grandma Deenie grew up and moved into her home with my Grandpa at the end of Ohio Street, the company built the park and planted sycamore trees along the sidewalk in an effort to establish good faith. Deenie and Paul's Presston became less of a company town and more of a 1950's blue-collar Pittsburgh neighborhood with the park, a corner store, and a beer garden where the men all stopped at the end of their shift, whether that was 6 a.m. or 6 p.m. Grandpa Paul's Presston was thirsty. It tasted salty and smelled like hot metal. It slumped, top-heavy after a day of backbreaking labor, wrung out like an old rag, damp and covered in a thin layer of grit.

Grandpa said, "I was content to play cards and have a beer after work, but your Grandma Deenie felt disconnected from the world down here."

I tried to imagine what Deenie saw: two streets surrounded by train tracks, woods, and the river—with one long road separating it from the rest of civilization. For Grandma Deenie, going *into town* meant a bus ride away from the river, up to McKees Rocks, where she could go to the beauty parlor or a grocery store. Traveling into downtown Pittsburgh meant crossing the long footbridge at the end of Ohio Street to catch a bus on the other side of McKees Rocks. Another twenty minutes further, they reserved that ride for special occasions, like the latest Gene Kelly movie. He was a local boy and Deenie's favorite. Every Christmas, Mom recounted the bus rides downtown with Nana Wanda to see the Christmas decorations at Horne's department store.

Still at the stop sign, I opened the passenger side window to get a better look at what used to be the company store. Later it became the corner store—my favorite spot for penny candy—with an old-fashioned, glass bottle pop machine and rocking chairs on the front porch. A warm breeze blew through the open car window and I remembered the taste of rootbeer popsicles in the heat of summer on those rocking chairs. I grew up and the old store became a bar—two streets, two bars.

After Pressed Steel sold the houses, the long row of mirror image duplexes that were once painted the same colors gave way to the individual preferences of their new owners. I drove on, admiring the anarchy of aluminum-sided duplexes with no attempt at being complementary. Grandpa's gray house with green accents sat to the right of Mrs. Carini's pastel yellow home with a mustard yellow and brown striped aluminum awning. The houses shared a wall and were separated on the opposite side by a dark, narrow walkway. The neighbor kids and I approached those tunnels with caution. There was some question as to where the light on the other side might lead us and a chance—a hope even, that the next time we ran through, we might come out somewhere brand new.

In spite of our wild imaginations, the walkway tunnels only ever opened up to symmetrical, fenced-in, postage-stamp back yards on either side. Grandpa's house was the last one at the end of the street with a little land to the right and a wooded area before the single set of railroad tracks that ran in front of the river. It was the only house without a fence in the back.

Mom waved from the front porch as I parked. Sitting on the old, rusty glider, her feet barely touched the ground. In her usual heather gray athletic apparel, she wore a matching headband to pull her short gray hair away from her forehead. As I locked the car and opened the gate, I noticed the golden flecks in her hazel eyes. Those glimmering golden eyes that matched the gold St. Christopher medal around her neck, the warm olive tones of her skin, and the pale pink of her signature lipstick leapt out from the rest of the gray-washed picture.

"Walking up to this porch feels like coming home to me," I said, leaning down to kiss her cheek as the creases in her forehead smoothed over.

"Jess, really? After all of these years? I grew up in this house and all I feel walking up those steps is dread. What fire will I have to put out today?" Her mind seemed somewhere else as she adjusted her headband and smoothed back an out-of-place hair. "I walked into this empty house with that same pit in my stomach just this morning."

"But you grew up here and raised me across the street..."

"I know it," she interrupted. "But I'll tell ya, as soon as I pull on to that industrial road, I can't seem to get a deep enough breath. The air feels full of dust. I swear it's worse every time I come."

Mom's Presston was a thousand arms pulling from every direction. It was her first marriage to my absent father, Aunt Sadie's highs and lows, Grandpa's doctor's appointments, and a garden full of weeds.

"Does it seem dusty to you?" She hesitated for a moment, then glanced down at the arm of the glider smiling. "When we were little, everything outside was dusty, though nothing like what Nana Wanda used to describe from her day."

In Nana Wanda's day, people referred to Pittsburgh as *hell with the lid off* thanks to the pollution of the industrial boom. The smoke and soot hung in the air and blocked the sun, leaving a black film on everything.

Mom stretched her legs out in front of her. "Nana would give Sadie and me paintbrushes and a bucket of water and tell us to paint the porch furniture the way our *Mumma used to do when she was a little girl.*" Mom ran her hand through the back of her curls and laughed to herself. "Sadie made it an artistic canvas. She'd paint some mythical character she created and get frustrated when it evaporated before she finished telling the origin story. I painted it straight like you paint furniture, and Nana Wanda would dump the dirty water off the side of the porch after we finished."

I resisted the urge to respond, hoping that she'd continue, but she caught herself and changed course.

"It makes me happy that you're happy at Grandpa's though; he just adored his Jessie girl. And I know what ya mean; nothing feels better to me than driving down the hill, under the trees, to our real home."

We moved into our *real* home when I turned thirteen and Mom married Mark. Unlike Presston, Mom's *real* home was in a neighborhood connected to other neighborhoods.

"I never see kids at the park anymore." I shielded my eyes from the sun and turned my face toward the other side of the street.

"I couldn't get you off of those swings, no matter the weather. When Sadie and I were little, Nana Wanda would shake her head and click her tongue, 'That park is nothing but sweet, colored syrup to wash the sour taste out of the mouths of Presston,' she'd say, 'but we don't forget.'" Mom turned toward the park for a moment, then back to me. "I stopped in next door to check on Mrs. Carini. She looks amazing. I can't believe she's 88."

"Too mean to die?" I whispered.

"She's worried about us selling the house. *Your Papa is buried two months,*" Mom recounted in Mrs. Carini's Italian accent with her signature frown. *"You should sell to my Isabella."* I laughed as she continued, "I told her it's going to take at least the summer to clean it out. I wonder why her granddaughter doesn't just move in with her?"

"You really have to ask?" I said under my breath. "Isabella has a daughter. I'm sure they want their own space."

Mom shook her head. "Doesn't it seem like Grandpa's funeral just happened? The thought of going through all their stuff is overwhelming. God knows what he has up in that attic."

"I'll go up later and take a peek," I said. "Anyway, we aren't here to worry about that. We're here to tidy up the garden. Is Sadie here?"

From inside the house, her deep voice called, "Mia? When is Jess arriving?"

Just then, the screen door slowly creaked open and my Aunt Sadie floated out. To me, she floated everywhere she went.

4. DEENIE

No one knows my girls the way I do. Their story is my story and mine is theirs. Of course, I know what happened; I'd never let death get in the way of that. A conventional reader might consider me dead, but I live in the exhausted brown leaves of the oaks that surround my daughter Mia's home, clinging onto the branches all winter. I sing into the pitch of my daughter Sadie's laughter, pray into my granddaughter Jessie's exhale, and dance in the moonlight streaming into her daughters' bedroom. I'm the garden that my girls tend together every year—the soil they kiss with their feet. I keep the stories. Let me tell you one.

Sometimes when I want to remember my life, I tell the stars about my daughters. Like the Neruda poem, I see the moon in Sadie's skin. She reflects only light. Sadie isn't a name you say, it's a name you sing. I remember singing her name as I climbed the steps at Mumma's house. Sadie faced the sunny window in Mumma's bedroom like an angel blessed with the light of God dancing through her blond hair. She couldn't have been two years old. She chattered nonsensically to a shiny, white, ceramic statue of the Blessed Mother on the sill. She paused before she spoke again, as if in conversation.

When she noticed me, she ran over to grab my hand, pointing at the statue. "Mama Mary, Mama Mary."

I picked up the statue and handed it to her. She held it close to her berry-stained lips and chin, then to her chest and closed her eyes.

"Thank you," she said in her baby voice. "Thank you, Mama Mary."

I recognized something in her reverence that had nothing to do with religion. At two years old, she saw things differently than others. Sadie's lens transcends.

My Mia, on the other hand, lives a practical life. The story that she tells herself, even today, is that she's nothing like her mother. My magic is in her blood though. She's aware of things that others miss. She's always put together—not a hair out of place or a wrinkle in sight, and only wears sneakers—ready to run to whomever might need to be rescued.

Without me around, Sadie idolized her sister and feared her disapproval. Mia adored Sadie with more of a mother's love than a sister's—a mother's love and a mother's fear.

"She's a moody teenager. You worry too much," Paul assured Mia, who recognized her sister's blank expression and detached tone of voice. "She's got a rebellious spirit, just like her Mama," Paul said with a wistful smile.

Around that time, Sadie became less of a sister and more of a problem to solve—a do over even. In my experience, when someone arranges your life for you, the implicit message is that you can't do anything on your own. It didn't affect my Sadie though. From birth, she was a feral little thing, biting and scratching her way out, manic to wrap her arms around the world and ingest every molecule.

5. JESS

Sadie floated across the porch to hug me, with sunlight reflecting off her jewelry and glowing in the highlights of her hair.

"Jess, there you are."

A step below her, I wrapped my arms around her waist. "When did you get back from...where were you this time?"

I imagined that Sadie and Deenie were alike in everything but physical appearance. Sadie stood tall, lean, and tan with straight, light brown hair. She wore loose blouses, wide-legged pants, and long skirts that swept the ground. For as long as I could remember, she adorned herself with crystals and gemstones for power. Growing up, she felt more like a sister than an aunt. We caught up fast, feeling Mom's impatience pushing us from behind.

"Sadie, does the air feel dustier to you down here?" Mom asked, dragging her index finger along the arm of the chair.

"It's the frac sand, which is basically silica—terrible." Sadie pointed toward the river. "That place down the way unloads it from barges and trains onto the trucks that deliver it to fracking sites."

I cleared my throat. "Imagine breathing that stuff every day—right near the playground?"

Brow furrowed and fiddling with her holy medal, Mom interrupted, "Can we get started out back before the sun gets any higher?" She grabbed my hand, then Sadie's, and squeezed, leading us out back. "I'm so happy having you both together with me."

Behind the house, she wasted no time in organizing us. "We've got to get these old leaves out of here. Sadie, I already opened the shed. Can you grab another rake? Jess, did you bring gloves? Remember that infection I got on my finger? You need gloves."

I pulled the gloves out of my bag and waved them like a white flag.

Sadie's slow, deep voice carried out from the shed as she emerged. "Mia, gardening is supposed to be a relaxing activity."

Mom reached up to pinch Sadie's leg as she walked past. "If you were in charge, we'd be here all day."

Sadie winked at me, wrapping her long, thin hair into a bun. "If I was in charge, we wouldn't be here at all."

Mom handed me a water bottle. "Drink," she ordered. "What's Jake up to today?"

I reached down to cradle a pile of brown leaves up to the garbage can. "I didn't see him this morning. He took the girls out early."

Mom raised her eyebrows. "That was considerate of him, wasn't it?"

"To care for his own children? Yes, very thoughtful." I forced the leaves down into the can and squeezed, crunching them to dust in and under my gloved hands.

"Ouch," Sadie chimed in. "Everything okay with you two?"

Mom's wounded expression vibrated through the silence.

"I'm sorry, Mom. He was very sweet. He even got me a muffin and made coffee before he left." Turning too quickly, I knocked the garbage can over, spilling the leaves.

I took a deep breath. "I shouldn't have snapped." I forced a smile. "It just seems like everyone, including him, thinks he's doing me a favor by keeping the girls—touchy subject, I guess." I softened my eyes and smiled more naturally to relieve their anxiety, but I knew, from the way Mom inhaled sharply, to prepare for a lecture.

She crouched down to wipe soil off of her pristine, white tennis shoes. "Jess, I know this isn't an easy job, but you blink and it's over. You should check in with Jake, make sure everything is okay at work. Maybe there are things you don't understand that make it more difficult for him to help out right now." She tilted her head and focused on my eyes. "You are the glue."

Wanting it to end, I put my head down and raked leaves toward me with my hands. "Everything is fine, Mom...just life."

Taking my cue, Sadie walked over to me and laid her rake down on the ground beside my knee. "This gorgeous, thick hair; I'd kill for it." She grabbed a handful of my hair and pulled it together, loosely braiding as she spoke. "Jess love, let's get you out into the world soon. Why don't you join me on my next trip? There's a conference in Arizona in a few months. I think it would be good for you. You seem a little...stifled."

Something about the word *stifled* landed hard in my body. I waited for her to finish and deflated onto the ground.

"What kind of conference?" Mom asked, shaking her head. "I'm not entirely sure what it is you do."

Sadie pushed her sleeves up, revealing long, toned arms. With her hair in a bun, she reminded me of a ballerina, swaying from corner to corner. "I help companies unlock the potential of their employees. This is our yearly conference."

Mom cocked her head. "That doesn't sound like a real job."

Sadie laughed. "You know that I'd never make it in anything you'd consider a real job, Mia."

Mom sighed and got up to drag a garbage can of leaves toward the woods.

I imagined hiking through the foothills of a mountain dotted with saguaros. "I suppose motherhood feels a little stifling right now, but many worthy endeavors are a struggle, right?" We sat in silence for a moment. "Right?" Sadie smiled at me warmly but said nothing as my mom approached. I pointed up at her. "Not everyone can do it as gracefully as *she* did."

"Gracefully? Ha!" Mom picked off the small leaves clinging to her sweatpants. "Oh how little you remember..."

"You never fell apart," I said. "Even with my father around, you managed to hide most of the fighting."

Mrs. Carini's back door slowly screeched open behind us and promptly slammed shut.

"Nebby old woman," Mom whispered.

"I locked myself in the bathroom yesterday, Mom. I'm hiding from my own kids."

Mom stopped raking and slumped a little.

Sadie approached her and said, "It never occurred to you that she locked herself in a bathroom one of the times that you would have otherwise seen her fall apart?" Towering over Mom, she threw her arms around her and lifted her up, making her squeal in protest.

"Don't be a *jagoff*, Sadie," she said, laughing. "Do you plan to actually do any work with us?" Sadie dramatically yawned. Mom adjusted her sweatshirt and rolled her eyes. "She's right, Jess. I definitely hid in the bathroom a few times."

I kneeled down on the edge of a perennial bed to pull encroaching weeds. "I don't know how to give so much to them and still...I mean, it feels like there's nothing left. Even the good stuff drains me."

Sadie frowned. "Just because you had babies doesn't mean you have to have all the answers."

"You had all the answers, Mom."

"I promise, I had very few answers and little guidance." She pushed leaves deeper into the can with a rake. "It would be lovely if life was only self-actualization and personal growth but the fact is I had a job to do; you have a job to do. We have responsibilities to other people that ultimately make us better." She pushed the rake down harder to emphasize self-actualization, personal growth, and responsibilities. She piled one last armful of leaves on the overflowing can and started back to the far end of the garden.

"These grasses need thinned out," she called back to us.

"Y*inzer*," Sadie said, shaking her head. "You mean the grasses need *to be* thinned out?"

The sisters were close in age, but Sadie had no trace of Mom's Pittsburgh dialect. In fact, none of Sadie's old friends had much of an accent, while all of Mom's did. Sadie brushed leaves off of her skirt in irritation. The emphasized words were meant for her. I caught Sadie's eyes to share her frustration and got up to follow Mom walking toward the woods with the can of leaves.

"Self-actualization Mom? Why are you so annoyed with Sadie today?"

"I'm not annoyed. I don't know what you're talking about." She shook her head while dumping the leaves from the can into a pile on the ground.

"Sadie's life might not look like a life you're comfortable with but it doesn't matter. It's not your life."

She slowly turned her head from side to side. "No. Sadie's life doesn't look like any other adult's life. I'm not sure if she's taking care of herself, Jess. When she doesn't take care of herself, things get complicated and I'm the one who has to pick up the pieces." She turned the can upright and started walking back toward the garden, speaking more softly. "Daddy spoiled her. She's flying around as if nothing can hurt her and it hasn't even been a year."

"If she isn't allowed to be her big, dynamic, dramatic self without you assuming it's a bipolar thing then who is she sup-posed to be?" I argued, just as softly. "We know what to look for and when to be worried."

"But we missed it last year, Jess. I missed it." She turned her face away from me.

"I know you're scared, but you're too hard on her." I stopped walking and she turned to face me. "Don't you ever wish you could trust yourself the way that Sadie does? I wish I could."

Sadie yelled, breaking the tension. "Hey! No secret meetings in the woods without me."

Mom smiled at me and I knew her answer. She grabbed my hand and we walked back toward the garden. I brushed my thumb over the tiny holes at the bottom of my worn through t-shirt and watched Sadie's skirt floating behind her as she ap-proached, shades of reds, pinks, and oranges swirling around her ankles.

I sat down on the ground near the garden, feeling better. "This past winter, on the days when the girls and I had nowhere to be, we had entire days that revolved around reading together, painting, and cooking. I'm grateful, even with the nagging feeling that I should want more."

Sadie sat down on the ground next to me. "I'll tell you what I think. I think that the sanctuary you create in your home is an art. The function of art is to validate the experiences of others and point to a higher truth. That's sacred work." She kissed me on the head. "But you should still come to Arizona."

Soothed by her words and presence, I relaxed into the meditative task of *cleaning the dirt*—as Mom called it, and picked tiny rocks and bits of leaves and sticks from the dirt until I could sift the silky soil between my fingers.

Sadie stood up and pointed at the house. "This place? Not art, I'll tell you that, Jess. It doesn't come naturally to create what you have."

Mom chimed in. "No, indeed. On that, we agree, sister. Canned food, dirty floors, absent parents..."

Sadie scrunched her face. "Daddy wasn't absent, Mia. What do you mean?"

Mom had already started walking toward the shed. "Mama's hostas are taking over this spot. Should I start digging some of them up so they don't crowd the flowers over there?" Her forehead returned to its typical creased state. She wiped the sheen of sweat off of it and ran her hand through the back of her short curls.

Sadie released her hair from the bun and pulled it smooth into a ponytail. "Is it time to let this go? Shouldn't we be clearing out Dad's things? It's been three months." She approached her sister with caution; it may have been the only thing she did with caution.

"They're crowding the peonies." Mom had an uncanny way of avoiding things. I got up to follow her.

Sadie persisted, "Mia, if you want my help with this house, we need to get started. I'm traveling a lot this year."

I could feel the tension wafting off of Mom's body and stopped walking, unsure if I should continue following her. Grandpa's death allowed Mom to keep Sadie close, which, in Mom's eyes, meant *safe*.

Mom turned toward Sadie and grabbed the scoop neck of her cotton tank, pulling it out over and over to cool off. "Dad just died. Can you stay in one place for a little while and live your life?"

Sadie's well of patience ran dry in the unseasonable heat. "He didn't just die, Mia. And what I'm doing is called living my life. I had plans before he died and that hasn't changed." Sadie stood up—her confidence rising, and brushed the dirt off of her knees. "I don't want to be pulling weeds in this cemetery. There's nothing left for us here." Palms up, with stiff arms, she motioned toward the ground. "It's time to let it go."

We stood in silence for a minute before Mom turned around and got back to work. "I'll clear out the hostas so the peonies have some more space. We can put them a little farther back toward the woods. They like the shade."

Sadie knew from her sister's tone that she should drop it for now. She crouched down to continue pulling weeds and I walked back to join her in silent solidarity. Sadie's Presston didn't threaten to swallow her the way Deenie's had, but it loitered with a similar darkness. Beyond the woods, the train rumbled past the river and Sadie watched it until it disappeared. After it passed, through the bare treetops, you could just see a barge floating down the far side of the river. Sadie put her head down and worked for a few minutes before she started telling me stories of her latest love affair with comedic talent, and in no time, the sisters were teasing and laughing again.

After we finished, Mom and Sadie took the last can of leaves and a few buckets of weeds to dump near the woods, so I took the opportunity to slip up into the attic. Walking through the kitchen, I found Grandpa's lottery binders on the counter by the metal bread box. I could see him hunched over the sage green formica table with a cold can of beer—his thin, white hair combed straight back, in a sleeveless white undershirt and slacks. He sat in the path of a black, metal fan whirring from the counter and wrote down the night's winning numbers.

I walked up the black, vinyl-treaded steps that lined the back wall, passed their old bedroom at the top that still smelled like his aftershave, and reached up to pull down the ladder to the attic space. I peeked my head up into the warm, stale air and glanced around. Climbing all the way up, I quickly searched through the obvious boxes but found nothing, not even the old pictures. I stepped around Christmas decorations and a box of old toys to get to the window and spotted Mom and Sadie headed back. On my way to the ladder, I stepped over another box of lottery binders and remembered Mom saying that Deenie hid cash from Grandpa. After Deenie died, Sadie and Mom made a game of finding it. I started back down to the kitchen, remembering the magic of discovering that two of those vinyl-treaded steps opened up for storage when Sadie showed me some of Deenie's hiding places. When I got to the bottom, I lifted the first step and discovered a thin, brown, leather-bound book with "Diary" printed in gold letters on the cover. I took it out to the front porch and opened to the first page to see *Deenie Kapala* handwritten under the printed: *This diary belongs to*. I allowed myself a moment to take in her handwriting and imagined her holding the book.

Dear Diary,   *August 3, 1955*
It occurred to me recently that if I don't create something tangible out of these memories while they pulse inside of me, there's a chance that the most important parts might be lost forever among baby bottles and laundry and lists of books I'll never have time to read. I tell stories. This is the story of me.

Even though we've celebrated our first anniversary, remembering when Paul and I ran off together fills me with the same giddy sense of escape. Before he came to Presston, I languished between those two lonely streets for all of my 21 years. I vacillated between thoughts that I was a mere speck of dust in the cosmos or the most important soul born. I read books about the jungles of South America and the streets of London, trying on different accents and methodically training my speech to elevate myself up and away from this place.

I dreamed of what might lie beyond the river or the train tracks, beyond Pittsburgh even, when he walked into the beer garden and offered to show me. Tall Paul, four years older, with his sandy blond hair, warm brown eyes, and strong arms. He grew up out west, traveled in the Army, and even left the country. When he lit my cigarette that night, I noticed he had the same rough hands of the other boys in Presston, but he listened to me talk with quiet curiosity. He didn't feel the need to prove his intelligence and only spoke when he had something important to say. And imagination! He had such a wonderful imagination. But most of all, he lived the life I longed to live: fearless and free.

We hadn't known each other long when he asked me to marry him. He had a car, some money saved from his time in Korea, and 3 weeks until he started at Pressed Steel. We got on Route 40 and followed it west without a plan—just the cash, his old tent, and Dick, an army buddy from Fort Huachuca, who settled outside of Tucson with his wife Helen.

I had no idea. The books that I borrowed or stole, the National Geographics that old Mr. Lenoski down the street let me read when I babysat...none of it prepared me for that trip. When the Rockies first came into view, Paul glanced over at me in anticipation, his silence affirming that he understood the space I needed to absorb it all. The jagged, carved mountains towered over us as we drove up and down at highway speed like a roller coaster without the track. A friend told me the prairie would be the most boring part of our drive, but I think it might have been my favorite part. The sun set over endless golden fields through an enormous dome of blue sky. At night, the dome melted into a deep black, trembling with stars above and around us.

The hot Utah sun signaled that we were close to our Arizona destination. We pulled over and hiked through rust-colored sand and soil to red rock arches. Sliding my hand down the smooth, carved rock sent a chill through my whole body. I imagined the arches evolving through time and the ancient people who lived and loved and worshiped beside them. On any other day, my skin pulled tight against the burning light of something inside trying to burst forth, but in the shadow of those arches, the big space that I occupied inside of myself became empty and cavernous as I shrunk to nothing.

We had the good fortune of beautiful weather and spent every night camped out under the stars. Far away from lights and people, we laid on a blanket in a meadow thick with fireflies and watched the full moon climb higher into the sky. Paul grabbed my hand and started singing "A Strawberry Moon."

He called it a strawberry moon—the full moon that made me stop and hold my breath, humbled. The strawberry moon put me in my place like the night we drove through Kansas, underneath an upturned bowl of stars—floating in space and insignificant.

"The strawberry moon is timeless," he said. "The earth is timeless, and we're only visitors."

None of it matters. No matter what we do, the moon will continue on its journey, the earth will turn, and it's perfectly fine if all we do in life is watch the way the light plays on the rocks and read a poem (or ten) and make love.

With every border we crossed, small twists and tickles unraveled inside of me. By the time we reached the southwest and the wild July monsoons, I felt more at ease in my skin than ever before. We pulled into the gravel driveway of Dick and Helen's late at night and spotted a coyote in the glow of our headlights before it turned and ran toward the desert. Dick and Paul greeted each other like long-lost brothers. Helen ran straight to me, speaking in a quick, staccato pattern that ran together at the end of the sentence, while I tried to take in my new surroundings.

"Here. Come. The Happy. Couple. Oh Geraldine, I. am. so. happytomeetyou."

Their house looked out onto the boundless desert, with an old airstream trailer down a path to the right where we would sleep.

After a late breakfast on our first day together, we drove into town to escape the afternoon sun with some shopping and dinner. In between explosions of colorful chilies in my mouth, I enjoyed Dick's warm expression and lined, brown face as he told stories about Paul, but Helen's incessant chatter was grating.

Later that evening, we gathered on a neighbor's porch to play cards as storm clouds bubbled like a potion brewing above the mountain top miles away. Just as the sun set, rose-colored columns of rain glided toward us as the lightning danced horizontally across the sky from cloud to cloud in an uninterrupted stream.

Paul caught me bewitched by the sight. "Monsoon season," he whispered, pulling me out for a walk before the rain began.

"You're. going. out. in. this? You're crazy!" Helen yelled. "We'restayingput."

They moved the card game indoors and Paul and I continued out toward a prickly pear cactus beginning to fruit, like a green spiky palm with sore thumbs where the fingers should be. Paul pointed out another with longer fruit like jeweled red fingernails so we ambled in that direction, further away from the lights of the neighbors' house.

The wind picked up, moving us with palpable electricity. We ran back down the path toward the closest shelter: Dick and Helen's place. Paul followed me into the dark of our friends' house as a force outside of my control animated my body. Giving birth granted me a more primal sense of myself, but that evening, I understood it only as an urge too strong to fight. It led me upstairs and out onto the back balcony facing miles of desert wilderness. The mountains appeared in flashes, backlit by the lightning, and ignited a desire within me to be entirely possessed. Paul watched me with the same desire. He wasn't surprised when I stripped down and walked naked toward the rain and away from the shelter of the balcony. He joined me. DK

6. JESS

"There you are." Sadie peeked out from the front door.

I pulled both legs up onto the glider and put the diary down. "I just read the beginning of Grandma Deenie's diary and it...wasn't exactly what I expected?"

A slow smile traveled across Sadie's face. "Ahhh...the Arizona trip."

"The monsoons..." I swooned.

Mom yelled from inside the house, "Sadie, are you trying to get out of finishing this too?"

"I'll go keep her busy. You enjoy." Sadie winked at me. "Want to grab tea after we finish here and talk?"

"I would love that." I'd get my chance to speak to her privately about the diary.

I decided to steal some quiet time with a walk to the beer garden. Empty swings in the wind whined from the lonely playground as I passed the fences of each front yard on Ohio Street: some painted a shimmering silver, others dark green or white. Each owner used their front porches or the hundred square feet of their front yards to differentiate their homes. A ceramic angel greeted me three houses down, with an American flag waving above its head and two ceramic squirrels plotting in the corner. A Pittsburgh Steelers flag flew out from one porch, near a black and gold mailbox, over a yard littered with colorful, plastic easter eggs. Two doors down, the porch railing had a line of ceramic knick-knacks from one end to the other: a pumpkin, a puppy, an angel, and three monkeys hearing, seeing, and speaking no evil.

One thing many of the front yards had in common were the statues of Mary. It wasn't unusual in Pittsburgh to find statues of the Blessed Mother in a front yard: alone or surrounded by angels, amidst flowers in a garden, in a cement grotto or one fashioned from an old claw foot tub, half-buried in the ground. She blessed most of the yards in immigrant-built communities like Presston, The Bottoms, or my South Side neighborhood. My mom kept a small cement statue of her in the back yard by the bird bath. It reminded her of Nana Wanda.

Further toward the end of Ohio Street, I arrived at my destination—the nondescript, red brick building that housed some of my favorite childhood memories. *My* Presston was a jukebox and ginger ale Presston. As a child, if I caught Grandpa on his way to the beer garden, I'd run out and grab his hand knowing that he'd never deny me. Looking inside through the one, tiny window, it resembled any other neighborhood pub: dimly lit, with a bar, long tables, and booths lining the wall. Grandpa said that the old owners used to plant flowers in pots outside the door, but that was as close as it came to a garden. A German family from The Bottoms opened it long before Grandpa's time and called it a beer garden, so that's what everyone else called it forevermore, even after ownership changed hands.

Around Pittsburgh, most mill and factory towns had neighborhood bars on every corner. In my neighborhood in the city, mill workers had to climb steep sets of steps to get to their homes dotting the great hill that rose up from the mill by the river. The bars on the corners were stopping points for the men to rest as they made their way home at the end of a long shift.

When we lived in Presston, Mom took me to church every Sunday to offer me what she found at St. Mary's with Nana Wanda, but I found it at the beer garden with Grandpa. Through songs and stories, he peeled back the curtain on our mysterious, mystical matriarch and the extraordinary love from which I descended.

He gave me change for the jukebox that only played old songs and ordered me a ginger ale and pretzels. I usually played *Tie a Yellow Ribbon 'Round the Old Oak Tree* first—our special song. Climbing up with his help, I twisted on the squeaky stool, swinging my legs back and forth, and listened to his memories.

I would often find Grandpa humming *Blue Gardenia*, the song he used to sing to her, his beautiful Gardenia—not movie star beautiful but authentically so, with bright, blue eyes and dark brown hair. He told me that she kept it pinned up during the day but in the evenings, the curls fell past her shoulders—wavy and wild, and her blue eyes pierced through the lengths of it. He had a picture of the two of them when they were dating in a booth with their friends—her reflection in the mirror to her right. She held a cigarette, with drinks littering the table and laughter lighting up everyone's faces. That was my mom's favorite picture, because she never knew her mother that way. She saw her tired, dazed, numb; she saw her contrite, guilty, sad; she saw her wild, passionate, fierce, but never easy in herself—never laughter in her eyes.

His Deenie wore red lipstick and drank gin and tonics. She loved Billie Holiday. She had a solid, curvy figure under those conservative dresses with her top button left open. At the corner bar with her friends, she usually had a book in her purse. Deenie babysat for a family in Presston whose walls were lined with bookcases. Grandpa told me that old Mrs. Lanoski's father left her an impressive collection of literature and she loaned Deenie any book that she wanted to read.

"I bet your Grandma read every book in that house from Dickens to Jane Austen to Henry David Thoreau," he declared with pride.

At a certain point of nearly every afternoon we spent together at the bar, Grandpa would get that look on his face and I settled in for the story.

"My first night here, the other girls were so loud, laughing and cooing all around her, but she sat there real quiet, in a bubble. I watched her from the bar stool while chatting with my buddies, but after a while, I had to meet her." That's when he would look over at the booth where they met. "I knew two of the other girls, so it was easy for me to stop and say hello. Just as I got there, the two girls sitting on the opposite side of the booth from her slid out, and I slid in. Your Grandma Deenie smiled politely when her friend introduced everyone to me but quickly retreated back to the faraway place in her mind." He paused to make sure I listened to the most important part. "Then, at exactly the moment that the song changed on the jukebox, she lifted her head and stared directly into my eyes. I actually caught my breath. I'd never known anything like it. She wasn't there and then she was, and those blue eyes burned right into mine. She said, 'I love this song' and flashed that mischievous smile."

A toddler wailing in the yard across the street startled me back into reality for a moment. I loved imagining that part of his story. Without moving her gaze, she took one last puff of her cigarette and crushed the end into the clear glass ashtray, recently emptied.

Still staring into Grandpa's eyes, she said, "Excuse me."

Her friends scattered and she slid out and disappeared. He just sat there stunned while *Blue Gardenia* played in the background. He looked down at the ashtray, picked up the butt—still warm, and moved it deliberately between his thumb and finger, rubbing the bright red color off onto his skin.

"Just like that, she was in my blood." He always ended the story with that line.

I peeked inside the old bar and felt ginger ale bubbles in my nose. It smelled exactly the same as I remembered, though it was dark and silent inside. I didn't recognize the old man at the bar so I turned and made my way back up the street to the house.

Sadie hauled a box out to her car and waved me over. "Hey, actually, how do you feel about Chinese food? I'm starving."

I nodded. "Perfect."

7. MIA

Of course, on a day like today you'd be waiting for me on the hammock—eyes closed and nose in the air like our old floppy-eared dog, Biz. That dog loved this porch, though his sniffing was more ecstatic than yours. Nothing brought him more visceral pleasure than lying here immersed in whatever the wind delivered, whether it be the early morning sweetness of donuts fried in the shop on the corner or freshly cut grass from across the street. That fat, ginger mutt lifted and waved his pink nose in the air while the aromas tickled every cell on the journey through his body, until the tip of his tail twitched.

I had a productive day with Jess and Sadie. We had to redd up the garden to split and transplant some things next week. We cleared out the dead leaves, cut down the spent grasses, and dumped it all *dahn the tracks*. The girls went out to eat but I grabbed a hoagie from that place in McKees Rocks to have dinner with you.

Mia, Mia, Mia—imagining my dead dog and talking to my dead husband. Biz is long gone yet here you are swaying in the spring breeze, opening your eyes to watch the crows fly over our front yard to the woods. One, two, three crows you count. You spent so much time in that hammock toward the end. I resisted the urge to bring you a pillow or adjust your feet, knowing how you loved your quiet time there.

Remember when the great *crescendo of caws* descended on the woods every September? The second year that a whole murder of crows came, Sadie searched the obituaries of the people who lived in our house before we bought it. How proud she was to tell us that not one but two people died in this house in the month of September. She called the crows' yearly ritual *the consecration of the woods*. You called it the *crescendo of caws*. There's that smile, eyes closed again, lifting your face to receive soaring, playful crow blessings.

Yes, if I have trouble finding ya, I'll check the hammock. Of course, you agree; you were always so agreeable. Imagine—you met me as a single mom, after a failed marriage. Determined to get it right after your own divorce, you loved Jessie from the start and moved us out of Presston and into our beautiful home under the oaks. You waited too long to start all that therapy with your ex-wife; you told me you'd already grown too far apart before you even began.

It's not easy to love people as they change. Remember my old friend, Elizabeth, with the shiny hair and the big bull mastiff...what was his name? I can't remember his name. You always tried to get out of dinner with the sarcastic husband. Neither one of us enjoyed their quiet jabs at each other; the *jokes* felt like a window into a house that didn't belong to us and we had no business looking inside.

Then you and I had a rough patch and Elizabeth told me how lucky I was to have a spouse who'd agree to therapy. I never thought of it as luck, but your commitment to the work made me love you even more. The therapist told me that I needed to stop taking responsibility for everyone's emotions. Well, that's still a struggle. Go ahead and laugh. But I did make some headway, didn't I? I stopped asking you if you were okay and waited for you to tell *me* if you needed to talk. I started enjoying our parties instead of looking at who seemed bored or drank too much.

Elizabeth with the shiny hair told me once that she was happy that the changes I made were alleviating my anxiety but she couldn't help but wish—*selfishly*, she added as a disclaimer, that I hadn't changed. She liked having a friend who did all the work. She laughed when she said that, like there was something clever about her honesty.

Her villainous laughter was such a contrast to your response. Sure, in the past, my irrational fears shaped our days, but my anxious heart looked three steps ahead of you to fix problems before you discovered them. I swept your path and rolled a carpet out so you'd be more comfortable as you walked. Then, out of nowhere, I pulled the carpet right out from under your feet. You stood there, toes digging into hard gravel, near broken glass, freezing in snow or sinking in mud. You just smiled, like you're smiling right now, so happy to see me at ease. That's love.

You used to drive me crazy with the therapy speak, but of course, I appreciated when you checked in with my *emotional capacity*. There's that musical laugh, like notes going up and back down a scale. It's the first thing I loved about you. You caught my quiet attempts at humor, and if *you* were laughing, it was funny. You'd never laugh to be polite—like that one Principal I worked for, who never smiled. When she complimented you, she meant it. That's the kind of person I want to be now. It took a while after you died to find my footing, but something is lifting. It's time to think about the kind of person I want to be for this next part.

8. JESS

After Mom locked up the house, she hugged Sadie for a little longer than she typically would—her way of apologizing. Sadie pulled her in with a magnanimous smile. We asked Mom to join us for dinner, but she had other plans.

I drove down the long road, grateful that Sadie and I could talk before I read any more of the diary. At the restaurant, we drank oolong tea and caught up on our summer plans.

"I wanted to talk to you about Grandma Deenie's diary." My knee bounced furiously.

"I can't believe you haven't read it before." She reached her hand across the table and patted my wrist in a comforting way, the bells on her bracelet hitting the table. "I understand what it's like to want to know her. After she died, no one would talk about her. Finding the diary lifted me up in a very dark time and helped me paint a picture of her, outside of the mother I re-membered. She died before I captured her as anything else." She gracefully swung her cloth napkin out and laid it over her lap. "'Mama got sick. Mama had to leave us.' That's all anyone would tell me. Daddy was lost in the past and Mia...well, you know how she is."

Cupping the warm tea cup in both hands soothed my nerves. "What did you take away from it?"

Sadie ripped open a sugar packet and poured it into her tea. "Let's talk about that after you've finished it," she answered, slowly stirring. "I don't want my experience to color yours. I will say that I think that some of what made her special has been passed onto you. I think that scares your mom a little, but she'll be alright. You both worry too much."

"She worries more than ever since she lost Mark. That last year, she was so consumed with taking care of him. After he died, she switched that same level of intention over to us." I looked down at my tea. "It's sad to think that my girls will never know Mark. He was so much more than a stepfather. He would've been a wonderful Grandpa."

"He was right on time for you and Mia, wasn't he?" Sadie asked.

"He was." I looked beyond Sadie to the sun streaming in onto the plants growing by the front window. "When I try to remember anything from when my parents were together, I'm standing in front of an oncoming storm: moments of eerie quiet, then a slow, cumulative moan from beneath the surface then a deafening detonation. When Mark came into our lives, we ascended out of the chaos and landed in some new place," I took a long sip of my tea, "where the weather was less volatile." I had to laugh, hearing my translation for Sadie, as if she wouldn't understand unless I spoke her language.

Sadie leaned toward me. "Did she ever tell you that she talks to him?"

"To Mark? To his ghost?" That was news to me.

Sadie patted my hand again. "To his spirit! I think it's good for her. She feels him in the house with her...on the front porch, especially. I think it's helping her work some things out."

After our waiter brought the check, I unwrapped my fortune cookie and read out loud, "*You will emerge victorious from the maze you've been traveling in.* Well, that's a bit loaded. I mean, which maze: the current maze of *my* life or *the larger one of existence?*" We laughed together over our tea while the waiter cleared our lunch dishes.

"Did you ever think that your concern with *the larger maze of existence* might be the source of some of this anxiety? Relax, Jessie." Sadie winked and squeezed my hand. "You're marvelous."

After lunch, she floated out of the restaurant and off to shower and meet friends at a concert. I drove home, jealous of her carefree life, but definitely a little lighter from the time in her presence.

Back at home, I retrieved the fortune from my purse and read it again. I decided once and for all that it meant the maze of my life. It gave me comfort to see the word victorious on the small slip of paper. I would not emerge intact, or better off, but *victorious.* I walked into the kitchen and placed it on the refrigerator with a magnet so that every evening while I chopped and diced, I'd remember that no matter how it all ends, I would emerge victorious.

Through the kitchen window, I watched my daughters play with Jake and the neighbor kids in the back yard. Instead of walking through the back door to greet them, I stayed inside to prep their dinner and ride the wave of freedom a bit longer. I turned my music up and poured a glass of wine, relieved to be out of my head and in my body. Sadie had that effect on me. Jake would hear the music and know that I arrived if he needed a break, but the girls would be too distracted by their friends to interrupt me.

I started pulling vegetables out of the refrigerator. Hearing the drawer open, my dog, Oberon, came in for a carrot, his favorite snack.

"Here you go, King Oberon," I said, holding the carrot out.

Closing the refrigerator door, I took a moment to look over the other things I put on the front with little cube magnets: another fortune, a picture of a mermaid that Sarah drew with pastels, and a photo Jake took of me when we were falling in love. I barely recognized the self-possessed young woman in that photo.

Like the garden for Grandma Deenie, the kitchen was my place to be magic and the one room in the house that I confidently made my own. I covered the cracked plaster with Chagall pictures from an old calendar and sewed curtains for the windows with some sari-type material that I found at the thrift store. The vibrant oranges and reds swirled together in a pattern that hid my lackluster sewing skills. With purple, I carefully painted a spiral design from the curtains along the wall near the built-in cabinet.

Over the doorway to the dining room, Jake put up the colorful plate that my mom and Mark brought back from a trip to Mexico. Over the other doorway, I hung the St. Brigid's cross that a friend gave me in college. I loved the simplicity of the dried rush grass twisted in that ancient way and the different stories of Brigid the Celtic Goddess or Catholic holy woman. Or both? St. Brigid was a medieval nun who chose the only path that afforded her access to books and art. She created a haven for other women, surrounded by a hedge that men couldn't cross without being cursed. In my heart, she was both. The ambiguity resonated deeply. Intuiting who I needed to be in any given situation seemed like a super power, but lately, I wasn't sure if a flexible identity was something to be proud of or something to pity. I imagined myself a clear quartz, reflecting a unique light from each different face, but maybe I just shapeshifted according to expectations.

I walked into the bathroom and looked closely at myself in the mirror over the sink: untamed waves of hair—dark and peppered with silver, a single line across the center of my forehead. I looked tired, even after an uplifting lunch with Sadie. Compulsively trying to be better took a lot out of a person. Back in the kitchen, I turned the music down as Jake walked in, eyeing the refrigerator door.

"Oh, this is a new one," he said, leaning in closer to read the fortune. "Victorious."

The levity in his voice washed over me. After a day alone with the children, the tone of his voice set the tone of our evening. He leaned over to kiss me from behind, brushing his faded blond hair against my neck and making me shiver, as he reached for a slice of red pepper on the cutting board in front of me. I turned around and leaned my back against the counter to face him. His eyes were brighter than usual. He smelled like a man who spent the day chasing kids around the yard—sweat kissed by a spring breeze, with a hint of the mossy sponge where he arranged fairies at the bottom of the maple tree. Hearing our little girls follow him in giggling, a surge of love or hormones warmed me from top to bottom. I kissed him, conscious of making it the kind of kiss that he would think about later.

"Victorious. I love it, don't you? I got it at lunch today with Sadie. It's been a while since I've gotten a fortune that spoke to me." The girls ran inside and wrapped their arms around each of my legs talking over one another in excitement.

"I mean it's no *Pennies from Heaven will fall to your doorstep this year*," he said, reaching down and scooping Amelia up as she wriggled in his arms.

The sun coming through the window felt warmer as we recalled the February afternoon that fortune found its way to me. I woke Jake up that morning holding nine month-old Sarah and a positive pregnancy test. In a blur of anxiety, we took Sarah to lunch at our favorite Chinese restaurant—the one he took me to on our first Valentine's Day. After vegetable bean curd soup and lemon chicken, the fortune read: *Pennies from Heaven will fall to your doorstep this year*. I couldn't explain why a mass-produced fortune would give me so much peace, but reading it quieted my apprehension about having another baby so soon. That November, we welcomed our Amelia, born fat and pink, after an easy labor and delivery. I held her close to my heart, overwhelmed with gratitude for my penny from heaven and every little superstition that made life more palatable.

"Mumm...mumm Mama! We are so hungry." Sarah jumped up at the end of her sentence, snapping me back to reality.

"What's for dinner?" Jake opened the refrigerator. I was used to him being famished at dinnertime. He got so engrossed in whatever he did that he forgot to eat. He leaned into the fridge and I admired his shoulders.

"Oh, yes...dinner. I'm making risotto with asparagus."

He closed the refrigerator. "That sounds amazing," he said, tilting his head with that boyish grin.

He came over for another kiss before going upstairs to shower. I gave the girls each a little bowl with hummus and sliced peppers to take into the dining room and they got to work on a plastic tub of wooden blocks. I turned the music back up, grabbed the asparagus and held the purple-green tips under running water, tickling the palm of my hand with the ends like paintbrushes.

I held them, bound together in the middle, on the caramel wood of my cutting board and smoothly chopped off all of the ends with one swift movement of my wrist. I kept chopping them into smaller pieces, poured them from the board into a glass baking dish and marveled at them glistening in the sun after I tossed them with oil. I ground pink salt and black pepper over the top and slid them into the oven to roast.

I chopped the shallots, using instinct more than sight, and allowed gratitude to pour out of my eyes with the onion tears. I slid the shallots into a pot of warm oil on the stove, then swirled in the rice with my wooden spoon. The nutty smell of the arborio kissing the oil floated up into the humid air before I poured white wine into the pot and reached for my glass of red.

"To Deenie and her magic—from her soil to my hands, from my heart to this food."

9. MIA

You used to say that the sky behind our house blushed with pride when I woke up early—how I miss your teasing. I had to stop myself from pouring your coffee this morning, Mark. It used to be my only motivation to get out of bed at this hour. I'd smell the coffee and know that if I didn't hurry, I'd miss our time together before you left for work. It's been harder to get out of bed since I started making the coffee, but the pink morning light feels like my reward.

I've been thinking about the other day with the girls and I'm worried about Jess. Something's off. It sounds like Jake is struggling, but she seems out of touch. And all of a sudden with the questions about Mama again? Of course, Sadie loves that—Sadie who played in the house whenever I found Mama outside smoking with that faraway look on her face. Sadie slept when Mama showed up in our room late at night—hair unpinned and soil on her dress. She was too young to recognize the way that Mama's breathing sped up to match her frantic movements in the garden.

Nana Wanda said Mama was *taken home to God*, but every night, I still saw her in the garden from my window. Every morning, we hoped to find her downstairs.

I can picture Nana with her soft, squishy arms, unwrapping her babushka and then the butterscotch candy she retrieved from the front pocket of her thick, scratchy, orange and brown dress. She set a small, wooden icon of Our Lady of Czestochowa on the coffee table.

"She's with the Holy Mother now girls."

"Why does Mary have a scratch on her face?" Sadie asked, inspecting the picture.

"She's a survivor," Nana answered.

Mama lived in heaven and Nana Wanda had no time for sadness. "No need to talk about that, Mia. What's done is done. You'll be fine. You just take care of your sister."

Nana had a certain expression that only Mama could provoke. She pinched the right half of her face together. The corner of her lip reached up to try to meet the corner of her eyebrow stretching down. The first time she looked at Sadie with that face, it made my heart beat faster.

"Head in the clouds," she'd say. It made her nervous when Sadie would dance around us at the bus stop or talk to strangers. "Sadie you are too much," she whispered, shaking her head. "Mia, hold your sister's hand and keep her still."

Sadie didn't know how to stop talking about Mama, even though I tried to distract her. Occasionally, Nana Wanda talked about her little girl, not our mama. Daddy would come home from the bar and talk about the woman he first met, but that woman wasn't our mama either.

Oh Mark, listen to me going on and on. The point is that the other day in the garden with Jess and Sadie, I shushed their feelings just like Nana Wanda used to do to us. Jess floats on the wind like a dandelion seed, afraid to land in the wrong place. Sadie has no fear, but she would say that her mama was flowers and pancake picnics. My mama rose out of her body and hovered near the ceiling. She sang into the soil and frightened the neighbors. She frightened me. Sadie didn't see what I saw.

10. JESS

I opened my eyes at 6 a.m. and reached across the bed to feel the quilt pulled taut from the morning before instead of Jake's warm body. I used to wake up in the middle of the night when he didn't come to bed, sensing his absence before my eyes adjusted to the darkness. Downstairs, I tiptoed past his closed office door, hoping he wouldn't hear me.

The little orange light on the coffee pot glowed in the dark kitchen. I poured myself a cup from the full pot and made my way to the back porch, easing the screen door closed behind me. I treasured the early mornings outside before the girls woke up, when the birds called to one another from the treeline on the edge of our yard. I sat down and glanced ahead in the diary. Some entries were neatly written, while others were furiously scribbled. Memories of ordinary days were interspersed with poetry.

Questions accumulated with every page I turned. It might've been the coffee but my whole body buzzed with anticipation knowing that I only had to wait one more day to get some answers. In the garden with Sadie, Mom would have a harder time changing the subject. I hadn't known what questions to ask before I read my grandmother's story in her own words. With each page, I inched closer to solving the mystery of Deenie.

Dear Diary,   *August 11, 1955*

After the trip out west, I saw the world with new eyes. Paul had to start work, so back home we went, taking on the last house at the end of Ohio Street. We couldn't have found a better house in Presston than the gray house near the river. Mrs. Carini next door spoke little English and kept to herself. She waved from the porch without smiling, a baby on her hip and her large breasts pulling on the buttons of her house dress. Her brood, too large to play in their yard, ran the streets and kept to the park.

The car barely made it back from Arizona, and I promised Paul I wouldn't drive it. I kept to our home for a few glorious months of poetry, sewing curtains, and attempts at Mexican food, all the while waiting for Paul to come back at the end of the day.

I knew that I loved him the night of that big storm in Arizona. Before that, if I'm being honest, it was more curiosity and escape. His intelligence and worldly perspective attracted me, and he made me laugh with his dry wit, but everything changed after that night in Tucson. All of my life, I searched for a way off of this dusty, two-street island with the fins of my mother's fears circling. He pulled me out of myself and into the world. He pulled me across the country in an old Ford.

In the early days of our marriage, we spent the better part of most evenings locked away in our bedroom and our bodies. We talked into the night about all of the places that we'd visit. I read to him before we went to sleep and woke up to his smiling eyes.

"How did I get so lucky to be able to wake up every morning in your bed?" He asked things like that all the time.

We lived those months with no expectations of each other. If he stopped for a beer after work, I occupied myself. If he came home to a cold can of beans for dinner, he'd eat it happily. He never asked me how I spent my time, unless he wanted to know about the book I couldn't put down.

Paul made life in Presston tolerable. He carried a different quality of light around him. He led me out of the hard light: the smoky shadows and blinding glare, and offered me the soft light under the sycamore tree and the rosy reflection of sunset. With him, a place that had once seemed inescapable became a temporary stop.

We talked about children right after the wedding. Although I never really pictured myself as a mother, it was difficult not to be enticed by his ideas. Once we were married, it was inevitable.

"A new person in this world, Deenie, who's taught something different. Imagine that." We'd take him all over with us and Paul would show him the stars and I would read him poetry. We could forge a new kind of life.

Of course, I was already pregnant before we said "I do," I just didn't know it. Of course, that's exactly what Mumma expected the first time that Paul's name escaped my lips. She ironed her blue, floral, polyester dress with the snaps, and shaking her head, said "tsk, tsk" when I told her we had another date.

Later, she sat on the porch in that dress and her sheer yellow babushka and told Mrs. Lanoski that we ran off and married because I "fell pregnant," but that wasn't true. I married him because he saw the parts of me that Wanda feared—that she raised me to fear. I liked the woman reflected back from his enchanted brown eyes.

So yes, after years of Wanda's Catholic guilt and shaming, I got myself pregnant out of wedlock, just like she knew I would— just like she did. I fessed up two months after we married.

"Guess what?" I lit my cigarette with as much confidence as I could muster. "You're gonna be a babcia."

She tried to act indifferent but her eyes betrayed the satisfaction of having been right.

"When?" she asked.

"In the spring."

"I hope you know what you're in for." She turned toward the coffee pot and poured me a cup. When she turned back around, her face was softer. She handed me the cup so gently that I understood she meant to communicate some kind of love or happiness for me, though she'd never say it explicitly. DK

11. JESS

As I finished reading, Jake's office door creaked open and the coffee pot clanged in the kitchen behind me. I glanced back through the window to see him—disheveled and agitated. I couldn't hear the birdsong and wondered if they all dispersed like animals before a storm. Jake walked out back to join me as the whining metal scraping of the garbage truck banged past the front of our house.

"Good morning. How was your night?" My jaw tensed with an affected smile.

"Okay."

"Did you get any sleep?"

He held the steaming mug under his nose. "Not really, but I'm fine."

"Well, it's Friday at least." The light in our neighbor's bathroom came on, distracting me. "Oh, tomorrow is planting day, remember? Will you be okay with the girls for the afternoon?"

He furiously scratched the top of his head. "I wanted to go in tomorrow. I need to do a good job on this project. Can't they just go with you and run around in the yard?"

"I'm not going to accomplish anything running after them the whole time."

He put his coffee mug down hard enough to shake the little

plastic table between us. "I don't even get why you guys are doing this; no one lives there. No one can see it. What's the point?"

I took a breath and tried a different proposal. "Could you stay later next week so that you don't have to go in tomorrow?"

"Is that what you want? You want me to be at work every night until you're in bed?"

I quieted my voice. "No, what I want is one afternoon with my family for a yearly tradition that's important to me, without spending the entire time chasing after the girls."

His shoulders fell. "I'm your family too. Why isn't *that* important to you? I'm working so much and half the time when I *am* home, you're off hiding with the girls."

"Only when it seems like you need space. I don't know what's going to set you off."

Tears pooled in his eyes. "I'm in the background, watching you three. I tell you that work is stressful and you only talk about getting time away from me? When do *we* spend time together?"

I tried to relax my clenching jaw. "So what you're saying is that my options are to stay home with the girls while you go out into the world and then stay home with you and the girls when you come back? That's it? I don't get anything else?"

He got up, pushing the plastic chair hard into the wall behind him with the back of his legs and turned to me.

"It's fine," he said calmly. "I'll work late next week and you can go." He started to open the door.

I stood up. "Please don't do this."

"Do what?" There was a terrifying edge in his voice.

I sat back down. "If you just say fine and go upstairs, then you become the victim of this interaction."

"And how does that hurt you?" He swung the screen door open wide.

I answered, "It doesn't. It hurts you."

"I'm fine. I'm not a victim. I'll work late next week."

He went into the kitchen and a moment later, a door upstairs slammed. I opened the diary, praying the girls slept through it, but the words blurred together on the page. I slunk inside to curl up on the couch, overcome by the familiar weight of slipping away: down, down into the rhythmic sounds of my body.

A few minutes later, I heard the slow whine of the girls' bedroom door. I held my breath, waiting for the creak of the top step and wishing that Jake would leave for work faster. With each startling slam upstairs, his anger grew into something more righteous and self-pitying. Heavy air condensed around me into walls of protection. The last slam was the front door as he left without saying goodbye. I jumped up to watch him walk down the street to the bus and took a deep breath, exhaling hard as he disappeared.

I didn't know who Jake was at work—if he released the tension of home and walked through the office door as the exceptional person I fell in love with. His coworkers probably enjoyed his great sense of humor and admired his creativity. I bet *Tracy from Sales*, who smiled a little too long at him at the office Christmas party, never watched him kick his desk chair against the wall after a stressful meeting.

I walked into the kitchen, filled a small pot with water, and poured dried oats into the pot as the water started to boil. Each small action in my morning routine took more effort. I looked at the refrigerator door and tried to recall the kind of hope about our life that shined through the eyes of the new mother who smiled back at me from our first family picture with Sarah. She imagined that her children would wake up every day with the bone-deep confidence that their home was a safe place. Instead, we lived in the shadow of Jake's volatility.

Putting him out of my mind, I hummed into the food, sprinkling cinnamon into the slowly thickening mixture. I looked up to see Amelia, giggling at my feigned surprise, with yellow curls spiraling in every direction. I turned the stove off, picked her up, and pulled a chair over.

Handing her a wooden spoon, I asked, "What are you putting into your magic potion, Amelia?"

Her eyes wide and appropriately serious, she pointed to the blueberries on the sink. Once I moved the container closer to her, she used her tiny index finger and thumb to toss one blueberry at a time into the oatmeal. Sarah shuffled into the kitchen carrying her favorite book.

"Daddy was angry," she said with a solemn expression.

"Everything's okay. Daddy's at work now and Amelia made oatmeal with blueberries." I dished up their breakfast and grabbed *Frog and Toad* from Sarah, hoping to distract her. "It's just us girls now."

After breakfast, we finished her book on the back porch before deciding on a tea party and bubbles in the back yard. As the sun traveled in the sky, I watched the clock move forward with more urgency and imagined blowing a bubble large enough for the girls and I to fit inside.

12. DEENIE

*Let me tell you a story. I watch from the budded trees and lis-
ten within the silky, silver catkins on the gathered pussy wil-
low branches in my granddaughter's kitchen. Jess heals wounds
with oats and berries. When her days are darker than usual, she
finds the color she needs in her refrigerator and sings and stirs
until she's feeding her babies rainbows. She doesn't see her partner slipping into the darkness, reaching for her. She just keeps
singing and stirring.*

*I promised myself a life with color when I grew up. There
wasn't much color in Wanda's kitchen. I remember eating dinner by myself at the kitchen table—must have been 7 or 8, stirring
the sickly, white soup of potatoes, translucent strips of cabbage,
and small bits of something brownish that I couldn't identify. I
dipped a finger into the stew then touched it to my thumb. It had
the same thick, warm feeling from earlier that day when my
classmates and I dipped our hands into the tub of paste all at
once and rubbed the chunky and smooth bits onto construction
paper for our projects.*

*I leaned down toward my bowl. It even smelled like paste. I
listened for Mumma in the next room and, deciding it was safe,
slipped out of my chair and into the bathroom, as quietly as I
could, to grab a piece of toilet paper. Back at my seat, I ripped*

the square of toilet paper into strips, dipped my index finger into the paste stew and rubbed it along the strips, layering them in a pattern like one of my Babcia Teresa's quilts. The low hum of the radio drifted into the kitchen through a stream of cigarette smoke. Mumma ate alone on the couch.

Every day, Mumma came home from working in the button factory, poured food into a pot, and let it simmer for an hour. She rubbed her tired feet, smoked her cigarettes, and listened to the radio. During the week, it was just Mumma and me at dinnertime. I ate at the kitchen table and Mumma ate in the living room. I asked to join her once and she scolded me harshly. She couldn't trust me not to spill food onto the couch. When Papa Joe was home on the weekend, we all ate dinner together at the table as if we transformed into a family when he joined us.

I leaned as far toward the door as I could, trying to hear her show. I recognized the program but the radio was never loud enough to hear what they said. Satisfied with my quilted creation, I peeked around the corner.

In that bone-tired voice of my childhood, she said, "Eat your dinner, Geraldine."

"Mumma, this morning I found a spider web near the riverbank that sparkled in the sun. It's like fairy folk blessed everything by the river. I think the mulberries down there would make a better dinner for me."

"Geraldine," she interrupted.

"Yes, Mumma?"

"Finish your dinner and take your book upstairs to your room."

I tiptoed past my cold bowl of stew and out the back door in search of the color I needed. If I got back before her program finished, she would never know I left. I never expected rainbows from Wanda; not everyone has that kind of color in their fridge.

13. MIA

I'm starting to wonder if I have some kind of connection with the dead. Last night, I remembered feeling Nana Wanda with me all the time after Jess was born. Once, the scent of her favorite soap almost knocked me over after Jess fell and skinned her knee in the woods. Then one day, it stopped. I don't remember when, but it makes me smile to imagine you and Nana Wanda crossing paths in the spirit world, now that you're my guardian angel.

I don't know what we'd have done without Nana Wanda, even before Mama died. Our days with her were safe and familiar—daily mass and a quick stop at the bakery or an afternoon at the knitting circle with her friends in the neighborhood. We never had to wait for her to pick us up because she always arrived early. She let us play dress up with her scarves and kept our favorite treats in the kitchen. She never disappeared behind her eyes or hovered outside of her body.

She rarely spoke about her parents, mentioning that Tata was quiet and kept to himself.

I asked about her mother. "Does your Mama Teresa live in heaven too?"

Nana Wanda shook her head. "God's mercy has no limit, but I couldn't say for sure."

I like to think about what Nana Wanda might have dreamed for her life as a young woman. In reality, it didn't matter what she dreamed for herself, because she fell in love or lust with a young man who disappeared when she discovered they were expecting a baby. Nana Wanda, alone with a baby in 1933, got a job in a button factory and found a good man—Papa Joe, to help her raise Deenie.

I never met Papa Joe; he died before I was born. It seemed curious that no one—not even Nana Wanda or Mama, had much to say about him, other than *he was a good man*. He and Nana grew up together and got married after he returned from the war. Nana moved from her parents' home to Papa Joe's home, down the street in Presston. Once, I asked her why she didn't have any more children.

"Can't. They took out the parts that hold the baby when Geraldine was born," she answered matter-of-factly. "She wouldn't be born. Your mumma was too much from the very start."

She shook her head and laughed, telling me that the nurses left her alone in pain, referring to her as a *young jezebel*. She knew something was wrong, but the doctor wouldn't listen to her.

They told her, "You had your fun and now you have to face the consequences," then put her to sleep.

When she woke up, she learned that she had a daughter and would never carry another child. Her mother came to the hospital to see the baby and told her about the surgery.

Nana Wanda imitated her mother's broken English. "See what you did now, Wanda? No more babies for you. Ha!" Nana Wanda looked up at the sky then down at me. Half-smiling, she shrugged. "Sad."

Alone in the hospital with her infant, Nana Wanda asked for a phone book and found a suitable last name for Mama's birth certificate. She wanted to protect the father from their shame, so Mama had a stranger's last name until she married Daddy.

After Mama died, Nana Wanda stayed with us in the evenings until Daddy came home from the beer garden. After Sadie went to sleep, she usually let me stay up and watch one of her variety shows like *Hee Haw* or *Laugh-In*. She watched television in the dark with the warm light of the TV illuminating one corner of the room and the glowing end of her cigarette dancing around her in the opposite corner. I would lay on one end of the couch with my feet near her lap and study the picture of Our Lady that she put on the coffee table. The gold leaf occasionally caught the light of the television, but I memorized her beautiful face long before. That Blessed Mother did not look serene. She looked like a survivor—like my Nana.

I don't know if the darkness made Nana feel safe, or the idea that I might have been half-asleep, but it's the only time that she talked to me about Mama.

"You're a good girl, Mia—so young but you take care of your family." She explained that Mama had a temper at my age. "I don't know what made her so high and mighty, but that girl thought the world owed her something."

She told me that Mama practiced speaking like her English teacher because she didn't want to sound like she was from Pittsburgh. She begged Nana Wanda to buy her books, but they didn't have the money.

"I brought home buttons from the factory where I worked." She patted my ankle and smiled. "You would love them. When Geraldine was a little girl, she'd play for hours with a jar of buttons—shiny and smooth, all different colors, wide flat ones and perfectly round little balls. One day I brought home special ones, thinking we might use them on a dress for her—like real pearls. Well, she wouldn't have it. She was tired of me trying to dress her up, she said. 'I'm not like you,' she said. 'I want more than Presston and buttons and tired, dirty feet.' Oh, that girl, where did she get her ideas? I never knew what would come out of her mouth."

She leaned away from me toward the tall brass ashtray stand beside her and pushed her cigarette down over and over into the brown glass as if to try and smother her emotions along with it. I tried to imagine Nana Wanda as a young girl like Mama, with dreams of a different life. Maybe I came from a long line of tender-hearted women whose fearful mothers extinguished the dreams of their daughters before someone else could—like

Nana's cigarette in the tall ashtray at the end of the couch. What had been extinguished in me?

Nana picked up her knitting from the floor beside her, gathering herself along with the balls of yarn, and turned back to the television. "Geraldine was too much...too much. I thought when she married and had you girls, she would settle down..." Her voice broke a little before she stopped talking. I pretended to be asleep.

14. JESS

Later that afternoon, the girls and I laid in their bed together and listened to an audiobook of *Little House in the Big Woods* until they were both snoring. I tiptoed out of their room and into mine, to grab Deenie's diary.

Dear Diary,   *September 14, 1955*
Mumma took the news about the baby better than I imagined and looked at me with a new kind of tenderness that was sort of unnerving. She surprised me with lunch yesterday and grabbed my hand before she left. It startled me, like bumping into a stranger.

When I was a little girl, I wished that Wanda loved me with the freedom and ease that some of my friends' mothers loved them, but the young girl who gave birth to me never experienced that kind of love. Love in her house meant food in your belly and a roof over your head. Love with my father left her betrayed and abandoned. How could she have known how to love me?

It was a complicated beginning, certainly as strong as any bond between mother and daughter, but human and messy...not ethereal, like the blessing of your long wished-for baby or some kind of covenant between you and your true love.

"Shhhhh Geraldine, you're laughing too loud." She'd grab my arm harshly and whisper, "Geraldine, play quietly, don't talk

*about that around the other children. Geraldine, you are too
much, too much, shhhhh."*

*Our life attracted too many stares and whispers. It seemed
like my very existence made her uncomfortable, but I never questioned her love. She sacrificed everything for me. See? Complicated.*

*I want my baby to have something different, like Paul said.
I want my baby to know that it's okay to dream, to feel, but
Mumma, even in her new tenderness, is right behind me, trying
to make me afraid to be me. DK*

My mom and Aunt Sadie spoke of Nana Wanda with so much
reverence, but Deenie's words painted a picture I hadn't considered before. Paging ahead in the diary, I noticed that the next few
entries jumped forward in time quite a bit. It reminded me of
projects that I began when I was pregnant with Sarah that moved
slower after her birth, before coming to a full stop once Amelia
joined us. It's a wonder that Deenie managed to fill the book.

I closed the diary, realizing the time. Jake would be home
from work soon. I walked downstairs to put on a pot of water for
the box of spaghetti in the cupboard. After our fight that morning, I didn't feel like cooking. I grabbed a jar of sauce and put
everything next to the stove, checking the window. He rounded
the corner toward the back door, with slow, defeated steps.

He looked up with a cautious smile as he opened the
door. "Hi."

"Hi," I answered back, trying to assess his energy.

"Can we talk upstairs while I change?" he asked, eyebrows
raised and eyes contrite.

Looking back at the stove, I willed him to keep his distance.
"Yeah, of course. Let me get this going and I'll be up."

Our marriage felt like a spaceship that we were both stuck
on. Sometimes being inside of it with Jake felt like a sanctuary.
Other times when I looked through the window for something
to grab onto, all I saw was emptiness. That day, I imagined myself
attached by a long, sturdy cord. When he passed close by me on
his way to the stairs, I stepped backward through an open door
in the ship and floated far away until I was a speck in the void.

I could float away for a little while, but I couldn't escape being attached to that ship. I just hoped one of us could figure out where we were going.

"The girls haven't woken up from their nap yet," I warned him as he started up the steps.

I poured the pasta out and gathered myself before walking upstairs to our room.

"Those work clothes felt heavy," he said, pulling a comfortable t-shirt over his head. "I'm glad to be home."

I attempted a smile.

"Jess, I'm sorry about this morning. I feel like I'm going crazy." He scooped his work clothes up from his feet and took them to the hamper in the corner of our room. "I spend so much of the day feeling resentful: hating the work I do, the people that I work with, resenting the bus ride home. Then I walk under the trees at the beginning of our street and see our little house and feel like I'm the luckiest bastard I know." He sat down on the bed. "Because I know that you're waiting for me, probably in the kitchen making something amazing that tastes like the way that you love us. I know your face will light up when I round the bend to the back porch, whether I deserve it or not. And I hate myself for making such a big deal out of this job, because it's for you and the girls and it pays for the life that makes me exhale under the trees every evening."

"So you get dressed in the morning, and start all over." The invisible walls between us fractured with my growing empathy and guilty complicity.

He looked down at his feet. "I'm sorry for losing my temper this morning."

"Jake, I don't want the girls waking up to slamming doors."

"I was upset. I tried to explain to you that I needed support."

I could feel my face screw up. "I didn't realize that was an option—to abandon self-control because we're upset?"

He stood up, his shoulders tensing. "They were asleep."

Something familiar in his tone made me want to lash out. "After last winter, you promised to control your temper. I don't understand how asking you to spend the day with your own children could elicit that kind of anger in the first place." Defeat pushed down on my shoulders and I pulled them back in revolt. "I spend every day arranging everything around whatever your emotional state happens to be that day to keep the peace. Still, I get punished for asking for one day?"

He took two deep breaths before he spoke. "Jess, I'm sorry. I really am. I didn't sleep and my emotions were out of whack. It wasn't about spending time with the girls or punishing you." His shoulders slumped. "I wish you understood that I'm not trying to hurt you. That's the last thing I want to do."

He turned toward the mirror over our dresser and moved his hand through his once golden hair, now darker and silver on one temple. "I don't think there's a solution to this. I just need to get my shit together." He tipped his head forward, noticing the thinning in one corner on the top. "It's the knowing that my choice in the matter is gone that makes it difficult, I think. What am I gonna do? Get a different shitty job?" He rubbed his hand over the stubble on his face.

I walked up behind him in the mirror. "I think you should do it."

"Get a different job or grow the beard?" he asked.

"The beard."

In the mirror, blond, brown, and shimmering silvers blended together across his jawline. I wrapped my arms around him from behind and exhaled deeply.

Something changed last winter. He stopped sleeping for days at a time. Then he started drinking alone in his office when he couldn't sleep. He worked later and later. I never knew which version of him to expect. Some days, he looked like a scared animal, unsure if he should surrender or lash out. I disengaged, held my breath, and kept the girls occupied till it passed.

Some days he seemed like a tantruming child, selfishly indulging his emotions. He slammed doors. He broke things. The time that he drove recklessly with the girls in the car because someone cut him off, I affirmed every ugly thing he thought about himself in a whisper. He lost it. I resented knowing that, like a parent and child, my reaction escalated or deescalated the situation when he felt no responsibility. I resented Sadie when she took his side and told me that depression looked different in men. My resentments grew and pushed us forward so quickly that even Jake startled when we reached the edge and looked down from the cliff. That's when he started slowly stepping back, and I agreed to meet his every step. Every time he took two deep breaths before speaking, we stepped back from the cliff, but we both still saw the edge.

15. JESS

At one in the morning, I woke up to a rhythmic throbbing in the side of my neck. I turned to see Jake sleeping peacefully at my side and took some slow, deep breaths until everything stabilized. It seemed odd to wake up in a panic after such a pleasant evening together.

Relieved that we were back on track, Jake was funny and charming over dinner.

"I think that bedtime stories should be a full-time daddy duty. You can get a little time alone," he said, then turned to the girls, "and I don't have to miss any of the story and wonder what happened to Ma and the bear when I'm supposed to be working."

After dinner, I washed dishes in the dark house with a flickering blood orange candle burning on the shelf in front of me and a soft light directly over the sink. Jake and the girls read together upstairs. Their occasional laughter punctuated the stillness and covered me in ease.

And yet, my mid-sleep, rapidly pulsing carotid told another story. I decided not to fight the adrenaline. Grabbing my white terry cloth robe with the blue piping, I slipped downstairs to read Deenie's diary. She began the diary with such energy but once she mentioned "the baby" the entries became the quick jottings of a busy mother.

"Mia likes when I read aloud to her but this baby never sleeps. I don't know how Mumma did this alone."

"Mumma took the baby so Paul and I could have a date night—how wonderful to be alone together."

"The older Mia gets, the less I see Paul and now there's going to be another baby. I wonder when we start his plan of doing things differently? Mumma promised to help more."

Curled up on the couch, I paged ahead until I came to the beginning of an entry that resonated. I looked to Deenie's diary for validation but finding it unsettled something within me. I opened a door and caught a glimpse, but if I closed it very quickly, I could still go back.

I decided to read on.

Dear Diary,   *May 11, 1960*

When I woke up this morning, a mother of two little girls, I watched the dust floating in the sunlight and thought about who I used to be and how to get back to her. Sadie came so quickly after Mia, I barely had time to catch my breath. All I can think about is having one week alone to visit the old me. I miss her.

I pulled on my robe and stepped lightly past the girls' closed door, but they followed soon after. I rose out of my body and hovered near the ceiling of the kitchen like those specks of dust in the sunlight: hollow, weightless, practically invisible. The body below poured milk into cereal and lit a cigarette. It carried the hot pot of coffee across the kitchen. Doubting the grip strength, I waited for the pot to slip and burn someone. A deserted body could not be trusted.

"Are you okay, Mama?" Mia asked, looking up at the ceiling.

The slow whine of the front door put me back into my body. It wasn't safe to hover from above in my mother's presence. I couldn't fool her. She wiped the girls' faces, grabbed their little hands, and walked them down the street to her house. She's been taking them more often. Maybe she suspects something about the hovering.

I unsnapped the pearlescent snaps of my housecoat, lit another cigarette and walked from the living room to the kitchen and back again, determined to use the time alone to accomplish something.

Maybe dinner? I remembered the spinach from Mrs. Carini. She would ask how I used it and I couldn't lie, especially to her. I found the strength to get dressed, knowing I'd be ravaged by regret that evening if I didn't push on.

Regret drained any spark of Deenie I still possessed. As a young woman, I promised Thoreau that I would suck the marrow out of life, but as a wife and mother, managing dinner would have been enough. Opening the refrigerator, I discovered the slimy spinach. Across the kitchen, the rotting potatoes met my nose before I opened the drawer.

I dressed and forced myself through the front door and down the street to the bus stop. I stepped around cracks in the sidewalk, imagining myself falling through, and over tree roots that crept into the sidewalk like crooked fingers. Suspicious eyes watched through the curtains of the houses I passed. If I deserted my body outside in the real world, I would just keep floating away into the atmosphere.

I reminded myself to breathe and ordered my legs to move individually. I counted fence posts to distract me from imagining my legs turning to rubber, bending like boneless bags of cartilage and fat—skin bags with dissolved bones and muscles floating inside. At any moment I might fall straight down, pelvis and trunk puddling into the sidewalk like the wicked witch of the west.

Three doors down from the beer garden, Mrs. B sat on her front porch smoking. She told everyone to call her that because her last name was a flurry of consonants that no one (who wasn't born in the old country) could pronounce. Her husband died in an accident at the factory shortly before he planned to retire, but she refused to wear black.

As a child, I noticed the stringy, white hair falling over her shoulders and imagined that Mumma and her friends didn't trust her because she didn't wear a babushka. I learned later that Mumma and her friends didn't trust her because she wasn't a Catholic and there were whispers about her helping women in trouble. She smiled warmly and waved as I passed.

I got onto the blessedly empty bus for a short ride to the market, but soon emerged into town like a newborn baby into a bright, sterile hospital room. I walked with purpose to the market, keeping my eyes down in the store, and scooped up 4 potatoes and an onion to get out as quickly as I came.

On my way back to the bus, I passed an old woman selling things on the sidewalk. Disheveled and absent-mindedly braiding her long, thin, gray hair on the side, it seemed safe to approach for a better look at a coppery bracelet that caught my eye. It reminded me of something my mother kept in her top drawer.

"Excuse me, is there a price on this?" I asked.

Without turning her gaze, she called, "Someone needs help, dear."

I didn't know how I missed the younger woman, maybe her daughter, sorting through a box a few feet behind her. As soon as she stood up, I regretted my decision to stop. The woman: attractive, maybe 25 or 30, wearing red lipstick and black cigarette pants with a button-down striped shirt, her long brown hair braided to one side like her mother...she was one of them.

She was one of those people who met my eyes and stared too long. Her face came alive, registering recognition, then determining me a stranger, it twisted with curiosity. I rifled through my purse, knowing that if I looked into her eyes, something intimate would be exchanged, leaving me vulnerable and even more exposed.

I had the experience of seemingly random connections before. Strangers stopped me on the street and tilted their heads, trying to place me. Did we go to school together? Did I ever work at Thorofare Market or go to the dances at St. Mary's? Sometimes, they would stop blinking, move closer, keep talking so that I wouldn't walk away. As a young woman, these experiences were precarious with the boys at school or the men at the company store after a long day's work.

When I got older, if I felt playful or curious, it became something altogether different. I could sit at the bar with four girls, much more attractive and outgoing than I, and the most beautiful man in the place would talk to me like they weren't even there. I imagined that my hips and breasts animated some evolutionary instinct. If only men were affected, that theory might've held some weight.

The power was intoxicating. I would sink into the experience, let it wash over me, and see how far I could take it. It turned out, I could take it pretty far if I wanted. I took it straight to a remote spot under the bridge with Paul three days after we first met.

I could take it into a deep friendship with the woman staring at me from the other side of the table that day—the kind of friendship where boundaries could be extended. It wouldn't be the first time.

"Oh hello. Can I help you?" she said without blinking, startling me out of my reverie.

I fumbled, asking about a price, and avoided her eyes.

"Oh, that? Oh, why is this out, Mother?" She turned to the old woman, who hadn't moved her eyes since I arrived.

I considered that the old woman might have had the same problem that I did and floated overhead near the thick umbrella of the maple tree.

"This shouldn't be out, I'm sorry. It's not for sale. We have something very similar though." She motioned for me to walk to the other end of the table with her.

I told her I hadn't planned to shop and was just curious about that one piece.

As I turned to leave, she pressed, "Oh, you have to look now that you're here. Look at this lovely bangle...copper too." She told me it would be like wearing a flower garden on my wrist. "Do you grow flowers? I have the loveliest roses behind my house." She stepped closer and asked if I lived nearby.

I pretended to look at something on the opposite end of the table from her, but she followed me there.

"The acorn bracelet..." She reached in front of me to touch the bracelet, the inside of her arm inches away from me.

My blue, polyester dress stuck to the small of my back. I babbled that I gathered acorns from an old tree near my home to decorate in the autumn. She stared at me with a strange recognition that pulled at the muscles in my thighs and down my calves. I noticed my bus approaching and said a quick goodbye.

"Wait! The bus to where?" The urgency in her voice felt inappropriate but something about our connection thrilled me.

I set my eyes on the bus stop and walked quickly, holding my grocery bag to my chest. Once the doors closed behind me, there was room to exhale. I found a seat among the other tired riders and closed my eyes. After reaching my stop and walking back down Ohio Street, I stepped quickly past my mother's house for fear that the girls would see me and want to come home. As I neared my house, I noticed Mrs. Carini sitting on her front porch with her latest baby.

"Geraldine, where is babies?" We were the same age, but she spoke to me like I was a child.

"With my mother." I looked up only briefly hoping not to engage any further.

"Again? Always with Nonna. Stop. Come here. See." She referred to the tiny human at her breast. She pulled him off of her breast and handed him to me before I could protest.

She held up one finger and disappeared inside.

What a day. I sat immediately, unable to trust my leg bones, and inspected the tiny baby. The child was all limbs and brown hair on head and body and couldn't have been more than ten pounds. Hypnotized by the soft, pulsing spot on his skull, I sensed the feeling from my legs had traveled to my arms and I wasn't sure that they could hold onto the baby.

I called into the house for her, afraid to stand up. "Mrs. Carini?"

She didn't answer. She must've been upstairs. My heart climbed into my throat and I couldn't swallow.

My body became a character separate from me, lying in wait for just the right moment to throw me off balance. Whenever my soul recognized the ambush, it evacuated my body and hovered overhead. To keep the panic at bay, I tried to merge my bodies—sucking the part of me hovering near the porch roof back inside to strengthen the body holding the child. The body could not be trusted with an infant or a hot pot of coffee. With the sound of Mrs. Carini's footsteps, my bodies merged, fearing discovery.

She approached me with two cottage cheese containers, each holding the small beginning of a tomato plant. "I have too much. Make food for the babies."

She put both containers down and took the baby from my trembling arms. I picked up the containers and started down the three steps of the porch, calling back, "Thank you!" I didn't bother asking questions or mentioning that I'd never grown anything before. Her off-putting demeanor and lack of shared language made things like that impossible.

I opened her front gate and heard the metal clang behind me as I swung it shut, took five steps to the left, opened my gate, and heard the metal clang behind me like the first gate's echo. I walked up the path, up the three steps of my porch, through the house and the back door to the back stoop. I set the plants down and took a seat on the cement steps, immediately relieved.

Lighting a cigarette, my eyes scanned the yard for the best spot to plant the tomatoes but were drawn outward toward the woods. We had more space than anyone in Presston, but I'd never considered a garden. I imagined picking tomatoes for dinner and walking down a path of flowers toward the river.

By the time I got back into the kitchen and put my cigarette out in the big, blue glass ashtray, the door opened. The girls burst in, followed by my mother. I went into the living room to greet them, happy to have them back home. Mumma asked where I'd been. She saw me walking past her house earlier so I explained.

Unconvinced, she hugged the girls. "Okay then, I'm off. Good-bye girls." DK

16. MIA

Sadie doesn't usually travel in May and June while we revive the garden. I imagine it's easier to stay home and avoid my wrath, but I hope there's a part of her that enjoys our time together. The only postcard on the fridge right now is the one she sent from Cape May last year–the vintage photo of cars from the '60s parked along the seawall. Near the end of the road, Victorian homes with elaborate porches in every shade of pastel welcome the people walking by. I keep it on the fridge because it reminds me of a picture I cut out of a magazine for my teenage bedroom, imagining the kind of place where happy families vacationed together.

> August 9, 2008
> Dear Mia, I'm sitting here with my toes in the
> sand and the warm water creeping over them in
> waves. I wanted you to know that I'm taking care of
> myself. I know it's as important as any medication
> or therapy. It makes me wonder if you ever wake
> up in the morning and ask yourself what you
> need? Maybe toes in the sand? Love, Sadie

The idea of asking myself what I needed every morning seemed absurd. Sadie went on about that the last time we were together, saying I could do with a trip.

"What would happen if you just got in the car and drove?" she asked.

My instinct was to say that I had too much to do, but that isn't true anymore. My list is dwindling. I remember when you used to tease me, Mark, about starting my day with the list.

"Okay Mia," you'd say, "better finish your coffee and figure out what everyone needs today."

For a long time, that meant my dad's doctor's appointments—and later yours, prescriptions to pick up, or new meals that you might eat. Then I'd move on to Sadie and Jess. When was Sadie getting that crown fixed? Going to the dentist made her anxious. You know what I'm talking about.

Once I ran down the list, I could start my day. At some point, it became entirely about supporting you, then dwindled to nothing after you died. At first, I couldn't enjoy the sense of relief because of the guilt that followed it. Later, the gaping holes in my day made me uneasy, creating space to live less in the present and more in my memories.

After dinner last night, I couldn't stop thinking about an ordinary evening that I spent with Mama. I didn't want to say anything to you because I hoped it would pass, but something about the evening heat made me feel like I could close my eyes and transport myself back in time. I heard Mr. Carini's lawn mower and smelled the cut grass. The back of my knees stuck to the glider while Mama talked. If I let go, I could have talked to her the way I talk to you.

That evening, the sun had nearly set. Sadie played in the wash tub on the other side of the kitchen. I found Mama on the front porch, smoking a cigarette in a pale pink dress—notable because she never wore pink and it was my favorite color.

Mama patted the glider next to her and said, "Come wait for Daddy with me."

She didn't usually wait for him. That, along with the pink dress, sparked my curiosity. She told me that she used to wait outside for him every evening after they got married.

"When I met your father, he wasn't afraid of anything," she said. "He'd walk along the handrail of the footbridge and skinny dip in the river in broad daylight. He bet his whole paycheck to win big and took me to see the most amazing things."

The Carini kids played kickball in the street.

Mama laughed to herself, stopping to take a drag of her cigarette. "Always singing. I loved that."

She went on and on, talking to me like a girlfriend at the bar. I'm surprised she didn't offer me a cigarette. She looked radiant in her pink dress as she described their honeymoon trip. You know what she said to me, Mark?

"I want you to experience all that the world has to offer, Mia," she told me. "Be brave. Be incandescent."

I didn't know what that word meant, but it sounded like Mama. I remember thinking that I wanted to be brave and incandescent, just like her.

17. JESS

"Who wants a margarita?" Sadie's deep voice sang out from the front door.

A moment later, she appeared in Grandpa's kitchen, a half hour late, holding a bottle of tequila and wearing a wilted flower crown.

Mom raised her eyebrows. "Margarita? At 3:00 p.m.?"

"Mom, loosen up." I grabbed my garden gloves off the table and smacked her behind. "It's our May Day kickoff. We should celebrate a new year in the garden, maybe our last year here."

Mom looked directly at Sadie. "It's May 2nd and tequila has never been my friend, ladies. I'll pass."

Sadie said it was because she never had good tequila. She put her whole body into mixing our cocktails, shaking and shimmying along to the music of her jingling bracelets crashing against the metal shaker and the tiny bells tinkling on her ankle and belt.

"Mm, smell this fresh lime." She poured the drinks into Grandpa's mason jars and floated over to my mom. "Taste. It's divine."

Mom cautiously brought the concoction to her lips, took the tiniest sip, and raised her eyebrows, this time in pleasant surprise. "That is actually quite refreshing." She took another drink and smiled.

Earlier that morning, I spoke to Sadie on the phone about my plan to bring up the diary. I had a suspicion that she intended to facilitate that discussion with tequila.

Mom took another drink. "You're in a very good mood today, Sadie."

"I'm in a fabulous mood and why shouldn't I be? Last night was Beltane. I stayed out all night." Sadie smiled at me, reaching across the table to hand me a jar. Mom rolled her eyes and gathered up her gloves and sunglasses. "Can we get outside, please? There's a *lot* of work to do."

I looked at the clock, anxious about Jake and the girls. When I left, he assured me that they'd be fine. Mom had nearly finished the margarita as Sadie poured more from the shaker.

"Looks like you have room to finish up this last little bit, Mia."

They made their way out back, but I stayed behind in the kitchen for a moment to look around. Grandpa's home was a monument to my happiest childhood memories, but reading Deenie's diary made it feel more like the setting from a novel. I brushed my hand over Grandpa's lottery binders on the cart by the bread box, smelling Bengay and beer. Peeking into the living room, I noticed his bowl of root beer candies—shaped like little barrels—sitting by the lamp near his recliner, right next to the remote. I tried to imagine what the house looked like when Deenie lived there. Hearing Mom call me, I turned back around and moved through the kitchen and outside to the back stoop, walking quickly toward the shed where Mom and Sadie stood talking.

We worked together for hours in comfortable silences punctuated by heartening recollections and easy laughter, until Mom lost her buzz.

She pointed to the corner. "The lilies need more sun. This has gotten a bit overgrown in the last couple of years."

"Lillian's lilies," Sadie sang.

"Who's Lillian?" I asked, looking down at the margarita I managed to spill on my shirt.

"Nobody," Mom answered quickly, anxiously rubbing the St. Christopher medal around her neck between her thumb and index finger.

Sadie's face screwed up defiantly. "Mama's best friend."

"She had a best friend? Why haven't I heard of her before now? Grandpa never mentioned her."

Mom repeated, "She's nobody, Jessie."

"Nobody, that Mama planted flowers for?" Sadie persisted.

"Sadie, let it alone. Leave it be." Mom put on her sunglasses. "This margarita has gone straight to my head. I can't do the Lillian thing right now."

Sadie and I knew to respect that particular tone, but I made a mental note to scour the diary for the name Lillian when I got home. There had to be an interesting story if Mom felt that uncomfortable talking about her.

I changed the subject. "Okay, why did Grandpa keep track of the lottery numbers in those binders? Superstition or did he have some kind of system?"

Sadie chuckled. "He was a bookie, dear—a gambling man. Did you really not know that?" She proclaimed it completely without judgment, as one would explain any typical occupation.

Mom adjusted her headband and smoothed her hair down in the back. "The police arrested him once before he married Mama for *keeping a gambling house* or something like that—running a craps game. Nana told me about it." She leaned over and pulled the tongue of her shoe out. "He started gambling with some army buddies and got a taste for it I suppose, even if it meant we didn't have enough food in the house."

"I never remember not having food in the house, Mia," Sadie plucked up the newly sprouted weeds between the roses and the lilies.

Mom turned back toward the bushes and kept trimming. "You don't remember a lot of things Sadie, and anyway, he changed after Mama died. I guess he found a way to enjoy himself and still take care of us."

"So, Grandma Deenie married a convict and a gambler?"

Mom laughed. "That's *exactly* who she would marry. Nana Wanda said Mama loved extremes. She was up high or down low and always had been." Mom started absentmindedly pulling clippings from the inside of the bush. "That *is* how I remember her.

I think even after Daddy bet the grocery money, she still felt sentimental about that part of him."

Sadie explained Deenie in her own way. "Remember the mythical selkie, Jess? Mama rose out of the sea to become our mother and disappeared again to be free and wild after she found her pelt in Grandpa's old cedar chest."

"Yeah," Mom said with an edge in her voice, "with a case of beer and a bunch of lottery binders on top of it."

Sadie spoke up. "She was a mystery. When she was full of life, she was more alive than anyone I've ever known." She gathered her hair into a bun and got back to splitting the lilies. "She was magic."

"Really, Sadie? Was that magic? To feel that light shine on ya one day and be alone in the dark the next? We were children. She was *nawt* well." Mom seemed more emotional than she usually allowed herself to be and reflexively leaned into her accent whenever that happened. She stood up, wiped the dirt off of her knees, and walked back into the house.

After a few minutes, I looked over at Sadie.

"I'll go check on her," I said.

She wasn't in the kitchen or living room. I climbed up the steps to the second floor and found her in her old room clutching a little pink vase.

"Go on and laugh at me. I feel ridiculous. I'm a woman who talks to her dead husband and drinks tequila in the middle of the day."

I sat down next to her on the twin bed. "Tell me about her."

She shook her head. "It doesn't matter."

"Tell me about this." I pointed at her hands.

She looked over at the window then back to the vase. "You know we'd go for days at a time without seeing her. She stayed in bed asleep or worked in the garden for so long that I couldn't be sure she ever slept. Winter was the worst." She rubbed her thumb along the circular opening. "At least when the flowers grew, she filled these little vases like coded messages. She snuck into our room while we were out and we'd find the flowers at bedtime like a kiss goodnight."

Sadie listened in the doorway. "And those nights, we fell asleep smiling and dreamed of peonies."

"The pink peonies were my favorite." Mom finally looked up. "Sometimes she'd fill the vases while we slept and we'd wake up to the smell of roses."

"Tell Jess about the day we started the garden." Sadie smiled at me. "Daddy would repeat the story every year when it was time to pick black raspberries."

Mom walked over to the window.

18. MIA

I remember the sky that morning, like God touched a rose-colored spot near the horizon with a wet paintbrush and pink spread out into the entire sky behind Mama. With a very sleepy Sadie in her arms, she woke me up and told me to follow her for a surprise.

She said, "We need your pretty pink bedspread Mia."

I followed her down the steps, dragging my bedspread behind me.

"What's your favorite color, Mia?" She already knew the answer, of course.

I followed her outside and found plates and forks, a bowl of canned peaches, and a plate with a towel over it on the back stoop.

"And what color is the sky, Mia?" she asked, like it was the first of many surprises.

It wasn't a sunset pink like I'd seen before. It was a pink that heralded angels. It saturated the air with wisps of cotton candy. I turned my head from left to right, trying to take it all in. Reflections of pink light bounced off of the sides of the houses and sheds and even the leaves in the trees. In my excitement, I started to run down toward the grass but the part of my bedspread that dragged behind caught the forks and swept them right off of the plates and down the steps, clinging and clanging the whole way.

I turned to Mama in a panic, but she only laughed. "You're making music with the birds. Come and lay that out for our picnic."

The light in Mrs. Carini's kitchen came on and we could see her slanted eyebrows through the window.

Mama said, "Don't you worry about her, Mia," and stared into my eyes until I smiled back at her.

She put Sadie down in the grass and picked up the forks, wiping them off on her floral print housecoat. She used her empty hand to help me pull the corners of the bedspread and laid the forks down on one corner. Sadie and I both jumped on. Mama grabbed the plates and handed one to each of us, then she went back for the peaches and the other plate. She handed the peaches to me and used her free hand to take the towel off of the plate, pulling it up from the middle like a magician.

"Pancakes!" She beamed.

We ate cereal for breakfast every day; pancakes were a big deal. Mama topped them with peaches and we ate in a chorus of songbirds—more birds than I'd ever heard before.

She buzzed all around the back yard telling us her plans. "This is where we'll plant the black raspberry bushes. Down the tracks, we'll dig up two—one for each girl. When we make pancakes, you can pick your own berries to put on top."

She moved from corner to corner, talking about digging up grass, growing tomatoes, and transplanting ferns near the shed. She pointed out toward the woods and described a path made of stones with flowers on each side. She promised a tire swing in the birch tree. She ripped up weeds and grass and started digging into the soil with her bare hands, telling us that the soil was magical.

I remember her movements, her smile—everything seemed exaggerated and it made my stomach feel funny. At one point, she grabbed the two sides of her housecoat open at the collar and popped the snaps open one by one. In her day glow pink nightgown, she unpinned her hair and let the dark curls fall loose around her shoulders. We watched her with eyes wide and imaginations whirling. I never saw anyone wearing a nightgown outside.

Mama sang and talked and worked. She said we'd grow a witch's garden with herbs to make potions for beauty and wisdom. "And maybe a potion to make Mrs. Carini smile more."

I never heard her speak that way about another grown-up. Sadie laid down to look up at the last remaining wisps of pink and fell asleep in the grass. I stood up quickly and felt dizzy—how wonderful and strange to be outside while everyone else slept.

Mama sifted soil through her fingertips. She told me to pick one little spot and pull any rocks, sticks, and leaves out of the dirt until only the rich, black soil remained, like cleaning the dirt. I sifted beside her as she told me about exotic plants from faraway places that we'd visit one day. The next thing I remember was waking up to Sadie beside me picking dandelions. Mama was dressed for the day with her hair pinned up again. She dug deep holes with a shovel for our berry bushes. Lunch was a picnic too: an odd combination of canned goods from the pantry.

"Mia, you are the Pirate Captain of this bedspread vessel. This meager lunch is the last of our plundered goods." Mama handed me a fork and an open can of baked beans. "Be careful that your crew doesn't fall into the sea."

Sadie dipped her toes off of the bedspread and into the grass and Mama pretended to be afraid for her life, making her burst into giggles. We pointed at imaginary fish in the grass and once we found land, Nana Wanda arrived to take us to the knitting circle.

"What's going on here?" The bottom half of Nana's face looked charmed, but the top half looked concerned.

Sadie and I talked over each other to tell her about our morning. Mama got up to carry cans into the kitchen, calling for me to get dressed as she walked up the cement steps to the back door.

We didn't want to leave but wouldn't dare say it to Nana. Down the street at Mrs. Ligenza's, even the apricot cookies couldn't capture my attention. I watched the cuckoo clock by the telephone chair, waiting for Mrs. Kosmatka to rinse her coffee cup and gather her yarn—signaling the end of the knitting circle.

As soon as Nana closed the gate behind us, Sadie and I ran ahead as fast as we could, but we couldn't find Mama in the house.

I remember feeling a little scared that Nana's worried look meant that maybe the day had been too good to be true. I ran out to the back yard and saw Mama down the tracks. Nana let us run ahead while she watched from the back stoop and Mama waited for us, pruning a bush to dig up.

"My pirate girls have returned! It's time to plunder some black raspberries."

Her hair fell in loose curls around her dirt-smudged face and her dress had dirt on it as well, with a small rip in the seam. Nana wouldn't like it, but it felt like a secret between us pirates. Sadie and I dug in the dirt with our hands beside Mama.

Just as we patted the soil down on the second transplanted bush, we heard keys jingling in the kitchen. Daddy stopped on the stoop, holding a brown paper bag that crinkled in his hands. Mama waved toward the bushes, explaining that she got the idea from Sadie's dream.

He got vanilla ice cream and raspberry jam. 'For our little Sadie,' he said.

Mama wrapped her arms around Daddy and they held each other for some time. That was the first night I saw her working outside in the moonlight.

19. JESS

The train rumbled closer and blew the whistle as it passed, putting Mom back in the moment with us. She turned from the window and slumped onto the twin bed. The weight of certain memories seemed heavier to her sometimes.

"The next morning, Mama didn't wake us up like she usually did. She told me she wasn't feeling well, so I went downstairs and poured our cereal into bowls. Sadie and I watched TV in the living room until Nana Wanda came and took us home with her. I felt like Cinderella when the spell broke."

Sadie said, "If we hadn't seen Mama for a while, the easiest way to figure out her mood was to look at Daddy. She walked into the room full of life and his eyes would water with recognition. When she couldn't be that person, the atmosphere felt heavy with guilt: his and hers."

"He was different after she died," Mom said. "He was softer with us and sorry for us. He drank a little less and sang a little more."

I couldn't help but smile, thinking of his voice.

Sadie stood up and walked over to her purse by the doorway. She had just the thing to end our day together on a hopeful note. Pulling out a handful of satiny, white ribbons, she grabbed both of our hands and said to follow. We walked downstairs and outside, just beyond the garden to the birch tree.

Sadie handed us both 3 ribbons. "Each ribbon represents a wish or a prayer. We're going to tie them to the branches. Let's set some intentions."

I stared up into the birch and pointed out a little nook perfect for sitting.

"Your ribbon would be closer to the heavens, Jess. You should do it." Sadie waved at Mom. "Come on, Mia, let's give her a boost."

"Absolutely not. She could fall and break her neck with two little girls counting on her." She turned to me, trying to keep it light, "Trust my sister to get you stuck up a tree."

"Mia, for goodness sake." Sadie's shoulders fell.

"It's fine." I threw my arms around Sadie's waist from the side, trying to ease the growing tension. "This is a lovely idea, Sadie. Let's keep going."

"Okay." Sadie reached up and tied her first ribbon around the lowest branch.

She prayed for a greater understanding of Deenie, that she found peace, and that wherever she was, there were black raspberries. Sadie looked over at Mom but Mom kept her eyes fixed on the ribbon.

Back at home, I fought the pull to check where Jake and the girls might be. With a cup of hot tea, I went onto the back porch to find out what happened after Deenie got home with Mrs. Carini's tomato plants, hoping that I might get a glimpse of the mysterious Lillian.

Dear Diary,   *May 12, 1960*
After the girls went to bed, I still had energy for the first time in a long time. I poured myself a gin and tonic, grabbed a sweater, and walked through the kitchen and the back door to survey the yard and plan my garden. Sinking into the evening air, I felt the absence of something confining that accompanied me most days, like dropping a heavy bag of groceries you've been lugging from town and running the rest of the way home unencumbered. I stretched my arms over my head and sat down on the stoop, then stretched my legs out in front of me. The air smelled clean.

I noticed random flashes of lightning coming from the west, lit a cigarette, and thought about the red lips of the woman in town. I liked remembering that I could incite that kind of energy in a stranger. She mentioned roses. Roses would be pretty out front—so much sun there. I heard a noise and stood to look up at the girls' bedroom window, but it must have been the kids next door. I finished my cigarette and laid down in the grass to look at the night sky.

Around the time the clouds rolled in over the few stars I could see, Paul's keys hit the kitchen table. He was drunk. I could hear it in his breathing and the way he smacked his lips as he fumbled with the stove, trying to light a cigarette. Usually, I'd just go to bed but that night, exposing him gave me a righteous thrill.

"It's late," I said.

"It is," he answered, opening the refrigerator.

I told him about the plate in the oven and how I had to scrounge because of our empty pantry. "Did you get paid?"

Thunder rumbled outside. He walked to the stove avoiding eye contact.

"I have some money. How much do you need?"

I repeated my question, feeling my heart beat faster.

"God damn it Deenie, I said how much do you need?"

"What did you do with the money, Paul? Craps at Tommy's?"

He walked toward the back door, throwing open the screen door to walk outside. I followed him, emboldened with reserves of strength.

Through the screen door I clenched my jaw and spoke slowly and deliberately, "Wake up your daughters, you big baby. Remember the kids you wanted so much? They need to eat. How am I supposed to feed them when you drink and gamble our money away? What kind of father are you?"

Something in his eyes terrified and excited me. If there hadn't been a screen door between us, I don't know what he might've done. He picked up the only thing he could find: an empty cottage cheese container. He threw it with all the power he had at the shed in the back, but the wind rushed through and carried it backwards, dropping it near his feet. Pathetic.

That wasn't the man who took his clothes off with me in the middle of the desert. He's tense and belligerent for no reason. He's angry about the children screaming from the park. He speaks rudely to the mailman or the butcher for the silliest reasons and screams at the confused driver in front of him who takes too long to decide on a turn. As if that wasn't enough, he can't provide for this family he dreamed up. I lie awake worrying about how to make the groceries stretch for another day and make excuses when Mumma asks why I look so tired all the time. I can't tell her that I'm afraid his job could be in danger, with all the times he's shown up late or drunk.

After a few minutes, I heard him come back in.

"Deenie, baby, let's not fight." He said with a forced sweetness.

He meant it, but only a thread restrained him. He reached for me but I shrunk back, repulsed.

"How much is left?" I asked calmly.

"Are we back to what a piece of garbage husband and father I am?" He kicked the chrome legs of the kitchen chair nearest to him, screaming about how I pushed him away and never wanted to be near him anymore. He stopped coming home after work because all I did was mope around the house like he ruined my life or something.

"I need to get drunk to come home and be with you anymore." A loud clap of thunder accompanied the flash of lightning outside. He stepped closer to me as rain came sideways through the screen door. "I need to let off some steam. I can't have some beers after work with my buddies? What can I do, Deenie?" He slammed his hand on the table. "What do you want from me?"

"I don't know who you are. You're not the man I married." I could feel myself separate from my body and float up to watch from the ceiling.

"Yeah, well I don't know who you are either. I miss my Deenie. I get glimpses of her but I can never get to her." His words ran into one another in a high-pitched whine. "And I come home and the first thing you do is tell me what a piece of garbage I am. I reach out to you and you reject me. Aren't you gonna say anything?" He walked toward me with an unhinged look in his wet, red eyes.

My body stood motionless and empty as the rain slowed to a quiet drizzle.

"You are so cold." He wiped his runny nose on his sleeve and I sensed the anger coming back. "You won't speak? You won't let me touch you?"

My body walked past him, up the stairs, and got into bed while I stayed in my spot in the corner of the ceiling and thought about the ways that I failed to be a good wife. How could I emasculate my husband by asking where he spent the money meant to feed our family? How dare I take a minute to process what he screamed at me, letting his feelings go unrecognized? Who did I think I was? Stepping away when he loomed over me, allowing him to feel abandoned when he needed validation?

He passed out on the couch for an hour then came up to bed. I pretended to be asleep waiting for his nasally, drunken snore. Long into the night, I laid awake in the dark, my mind buzzing with plans to disappear and become someone new. Whatever it meant to be a loving wife and a good mother: I failed. I had fifty dollars hidden in the step: enough to get me somewhere else, to find someone else, who would get me far away from here. I was no good for the girls. They were better off with my mother than with us.

I closed the diary before the entry ended, holding my place with a finger. I couldn't believe that the man she described was my Grandpa. Reading his words cut a tender part of my heart—a fresh wound. It sounded like Jake. I took a deep breath, a sip of my tea, and continued reading.

Then, with nothing but pitch-black darkness around me, I felt someone else in the room. Sadie put her little hand on my wrist and cried, something about raspberries, and begged for her Nana. I shushed her, picked her up, and carried her out of the room and down the steps to the kitchen. I put her down on the kitchen table and sat down in front of her on the chair.

Sitting rigidly, she accused me of leaving her to pick berries in the woods. "You were gone for so long. When you came to Nana's, you only brought me one black raspberry." She held up one index finger close to my nose as tears ran down her cheeks. "You ate them all. You didn't save any for me." She told me her story in between the deep inhales of her cries.

I told her it was just a dream. The black raspberries hadn't come yet; they needed the summer sun. I pushed the wet ends of her hair away from her cheeks and held her face in my hand, wiping the tears with my thumbs.

In a flash of inspiration, I told her to close her eyes, and leaned down to softly kiss her left eye and then her right. We would go out to the woods with a shovel and dig up a black raspberry bush to plant in our yard.

"Then next year, you can go out and pick black raspberries whenever you like for as long as they grow," I promised her.

That idea put some sparkle in her eyes, but she was too sleepy to talk about it. She hugged me close and put her head on my shoulder.

"Someone have a bad dream?" I heard from the stairs.

The regret in Paul's eyes and the feeling of our baby in my arms softened me. "She had a bad dream about a selfish Mama who ate all her berries."

He came down to pick Sadie up from the table and she cuddled into his shoulder. As I watched them walk upstairs, a wave of remorse covered me. Sadie went right back to sleep. We got back into bed, turned toward opposite walls, and Paul began snoring within a few minutes. My brain started to buzz again, so I eased my body out of bed and grabbed the diary.

Why would she dream of such a thing? She wanted her Nana, like somewhere inside, Sadie didn't trust me. She was angry and betrayed, as if she sensed the thoughts I had moments before she came into the room. What if this was one of those times when the universe tried to guide me? What if that's why Mrs. Carini gave me the tomatoes to plant? What if that's why I met the woman in the cigarette pants and she talked to me about flower gardens and roses? The girls and I could dig up plants from the woods and bring them to our yard. Spending time outside has always been good for me. I can fix this. DK

Outside, I heard Sarah's high-pitched voice and excited stuttering. I rushed to finish the raspberry story from Deenie's perspective. That night must've been the night before the pancake picnic? The sentences ran together in frenetic script. I grabbed a piece of mail to use as a bookmark and got up to greet Jake and the girls as they rounded the bend.

"Mum...mum...Mama! We went to the park today and saw three dogs and ga...ga...got ice cream and sprinkles." Sarah grabbed my hand and led me through the door and into the kitchen.

Jake followed close behind, holding Amelia. He kissed me hello on the cheek as I grabbed her sticky hand. In the kitchen, he reached up into the cupboard to get a new roll of paper towels and I ran my fingers along his right shoulder as he turned.

"How was your day?" he asked, smiling at me.

"Really great. Thank you for this."

"We've had a great day," he reassured me. He wet a paper towel and followed Amelia into the dining room to wipe off her face and hands.

"Sarah, let's go upstairs," he called from the other room. "I'm going to toss these girls into the tub, Jess. Everything's sticky."

I picked the dead leaves off of the second spider plant that I failed that year. "I'll join you after I finish reading this section."

He walked into the kitchen and put his arms around my waist. "Take your time. I can get them to bed."

"Thank you for everything today." I pressed my lips onto his and he kissed me back, pulling me closer. "Let's get these kids to sleep." I said.

"Let's," he answered.

He disappeared to the girls and I walked outside to the tea I forgot about and the diary with a torn envelope holding my place. Through the screen door I could hear Jake asking the girls about their favorite part of the day and their words joyfully collided and tumbled over one another until they faded away upstairs.

I exhaled deeply, distracted by our kiss. It made me wonder about life without the pressure of the family we created together and everything it entailed. Deenie and Paul's relationship deteriorated considerably between the Arizona trip and the last diary entry, but hearing Jake with our daughters evoked such a strong and different sort of love. Missing the three of them, I finished my cold mug of tea and went back inside.

20. DEENIE

*L*et me tell you a story while I tiptoe up the spiraling wisteria vine and shower myself in purple petals. It must've been four in the morning when I finished writing in the diary after Sadie's bad dream. Presston transformed at that hour: no blinding sun bouncing off of the concrete or mothers sweeping dusty sidewalks and gossipping over four-foot chain link fences. At 4 a.m., Presston became something hushed and reverent and unknowable.

"Come out," it beckoned from beyond the back stoop.

I pulled on a long rain coat to hide my nightgown and obeyed. Outside, I glanced over at the smattering of lights that revealed the back yards of our neighbors. Mr. Carini mowed his grass to a perfect one and a half-inch height. In a month it would be bordered on one side by deep green basil and spinach, and the other by bright red tomatoes. They had more children than I could count. Three doors down, Mrs. Brosky's overgrown grass was littered with toys and she had one little girl Sadie's age. Our yard was completely unremarkable. My eyes were drawn to the right where the budding trees swayed in the moonlight. The full moon summoned me off of the stoop like the lightning and winds of Tucson did years before. I recognized the familiar pull as an invitation for reclamation.

Moving in the direction of the woods, the energy of the trees drew me forward, like spotting long lost friends in the distance.

I remembered feeling connected to and held by the earth. As a child, I carried an ancient knowledge that eluded those around me and bewildered my mother. Somewhere along the way, I lost it, but I recognized it coming back to me.

Embraced by the darkness, I ambled toward the far end of the tree line. The bright light of the moon shot through the breaks in the trees and guided my footsteps to the black raspberry bushes. I brushed broken sticks and old leaves from in front of one of the bushes and kneeled down to inspect it. The jolt of a thorn sinking into the thumb of my right hand invigorated me. Bringing my right hand to my lips, I tasted the bright red blood, then scraped and dug into the soil below, forcing the cold earth through the soft parts in between my fingers. I felt the energy of the earth, like electricity, travel from my bleeding hand to my heart, bringing me fully into my body.

Standing up, I walked in the direction of the old oak tree and the moon beyond it. In a bright sliver of moonlight, crisp, purple blossoms caught my eye. Camouflaged by limbs, they wrapped around and around the trunk, one thick, long ringlet of an ancient Wisteria vine climbing sixty feet above me: a faint lilac in some parts, a deep amethyst weeping in others. I turned my face upward in the light and whispered a prayer of thanks.

Roots shot out of the bottoms of my feet and deep into the soil. I took off my raincoat and lifted my arms to the sky to make space in my body because I knew—the way that I used to know—that I was a channel for something divine. A Neruda poem fell into my mouth, and that night in Tucson pulsed in my trembling fingers. I raised my voice right there in the middle of the woods, in the middle of the night, and recited the poem, "If You Forget Me," to the trees and the soil and the thorny black raspberry bush that were my lovers that night.

When the light changed, I left my raincoat on the ground and meandered home in my nightgown, continuing the poem in my head. I washed my hands in the kitchen sink, walked upstairs to our bedroom, slipped out of my nightgown, and got into bed. Brushing Paul's thick, light-brown hair away from his face, I kissed his forehead. Eyes slowly opening, brows raised, he smiled softly at me with watery eyes. I climbed on top of him naked, never bothering to shut the door or the curtains, and whispered the end of the poem into his ear.

SUMMER

21. MIA

I n the muggy Pittsburgh summer, there's something intoxicating
about the early morning air before the temperature climbs—when
you can just begin to feel the weight of it. The hazy sky heavy above
the church and the hills beyond reminds me to enjoy this perfect
morning before the humidity permeates everything. It's Jessie's
birthday, Mark. You know how my body remembers—every year on
June 21st, my eyes open with the sunrise to a stirring in my blood
and a humming in my bones. It sounds corny but my life really did
begin the day she was born. How many times have you heard me
say that? You let me retell my stories without interruption—your
face rising and falling as if it's the first time you've heard them.

I drifted into motherhood like a raft carried out on the rising tide. Like my mother and her mother before her, I was young,
and it was unplanned. When Nana Wanda died, it felt even more
important to stay in Presston and look after Sadie. Jessie's father
worked at the factory with the Carini boys. I ignored the red flags
because he was smart and funny and made me feel like more than
my family's caretaker. When I got pregnant, we got married and
rented a house across the street, but Pressed Steel closed a few
months after Jessie's birth.

When the company closed, most of the boys I grew up with
hadn't made back-up plans. They were raised by steelworkers to be

a certain kind of man and bussing tables at Eat'n Park didn't feel like man's work. It didn't pay enough to support a family either. Tony Carini broke off his engagement and started fights at the Beer Garden every weekend. Joey Carini brought drugs into the neighborhood. He swept Jessie's father right along with him in a quest to escape. Jessie's dad disappeared for months at a time until he disappeared for good and I became Jessie's only protector in the world.

I thought that the pressure of being a single mother would stabilize as she got older, but it increased every time I failed to protect her. On the brink of Jessie's adolescence, dread hung over me like a dark cloud during the most mundane parts of any day—doing laundry or cooking dinner. With the windows down on a beautiful summer evening, I had a panic attack driving on the highway with no traffic in sight. I became obsessed with keeping her from an unplanned pregnancy so she could have the choices that I didn't have—that Deenie and Wanda didn't have. It was so much easier when she was a baby.

The first time I held Jessie in my arms, I vowed to never let my daughter feel as unprotected as I felt growing up. The urgency to protect my sister came from a place of insecurity, but becoming someone's mother tethered me to something tangible. Jessie was solid ground. What a relief to find that belonging and purpose, when I knew that it wasn't that way for every woman. I certainly hadn't tethered Deenie to anything good. Even in the chaos of my relationship with Jessie's father and our youth and poverty, I woke up every day renewed.

Of course, the feeling waned by the end of the day. After I nursed her to sleep at night, I peeled myself away from her skin with gratitude. Nothing sounded sweeter than the shower turning on to wash away a day's worth of our shared humanity—so much milk, so many tears. I stood under the warm water praying that she'd stay asleep. My heart sank when she inevitably cried, knowing that I had to surrender the plans I made and go to her.

Remembering it now, I see those moments as sacrosanct. I could close my eyes and be right back there with her.

Upstairs, I would push open the bedroom door, following her voice through the darkness.

"Jessie girl," I called over and over in a sing-song tone to calm her.

When she heard my voice, her desperate pleas became thankful relief. Short, high-pitched screams became a long, drawn-out exhale of song. She sunk into the mattress from the rigid pose she held in the moments before. I laid her down next to me on my bed, pressing my lips into the space where her velvet cheeks melted into the skin of her neck.

When she felt the pressure of my lips, she quickly turned her baby bird mouth toward me, then back and forth in anticipation, her breathing quicker and shallower, until she latched on and we both exhaled into the bed. She wrapped a tiny, cold hand around my index finger, and I imagined the warm milk soothing her like a hot cup of tea did for me.

Three months earlier, she floated in the warmth and darkness of my body, sleeping and waking to the sound of my breath, my heartbeat, and my voice. I had been her peace in so many new sensory experiences, and I realized in that moment how she became mine. I was conscious of her breath, her suckling pattern, and her heartbeat. Nothing else mattered. That must have been what the garden was for Mama; I never thought of it like that before.

Eventually Jessie floated through dreams and only suckled occasionally, her little body perfectly curved into mine. It humbled me to know that I had everything she needed. She gave me a significance that I didn't have before.

My dad adored her. When she came into the world—a fresh start, something reignited inside of him. Watching him ease into the role with so much joy connected us in a new way when we had been disconnected for so long. Sadie was old enough to help guide her but young enough to enjoy her.

And you know what, Mark? Watching her grow up made me appreciate things in myself that I didn't know how to love until I loved them in her.

22. JESS

I sipped my third cup of coffee on the back porch and watched my daughters play in the yard. With no breeze, the morning air felt deliciously sticky and warm. The girls ran out back in their nightgowns as soon as they finished breakfast. Sarah explained to her baby sister why the dirt needed to go from cup to bowl and not into her mouth when the phone rang.

Mom's voice carried through the receiver and filled the kitchen. "Well good morning, birthday girl."

"Good morning, Mom. It's a beautiful one, isn't it?"

It's a humid one—just like the day you were born. Do my granddaughters know they're going to the zoo with Grandma today?"

"They do. They're very excited about the monkey house. What time are you heading over?"

"I'll be there in about an hour. I love you, Jessie girl."

Mom's love felt like the quilt on my childhood bed—just the right blend of worn softness on my cheek and weight over my heart. Holding onto it gave me an immediate sense of safety, but on some days, I struggled beneath the burden of those colorful corduroy squares bound together with heavy stitching.

I relaxed back into my chair, feeling less clumsy than most mornings and content in the moment of coffee, sunshine, and my busy, curious daughters. It felt like a birthday gift from the universe in light of a morning earlier that week, when I sat on the kitchen floor staring into a bowl of oatmeal and Sarah wrapped yarn from my knitting basket around and across from knob to knob on the cupboard doors in a zigzag pattern.

"La..la..look Mama, look Mama," she instructed with pride.

I pushed aside visions of unwinding the reds and purples and blues dancing across my kitchen, thankful that she quietly occupied herself. Amelia rubbed curds of cottage cheese into the wood floor with her thumbs like we did with pastels on butcher paper. A familiar pressure rose from my ankles and I walked down the hall to the bathroom and locked myself inside.

I could hear my mother's voice in my ear, "Are you thinking of your daughters or yourself? You'll have plenty of time to enjoy a clean kitchen when they're older."

She used different words to convey the same message: I didn't matter as much as everyone else and it was selfish to put my needs before my family's. With two precious minutes of quiet, I took shelter in the tub and pulled the curtain before the girls started banging on the door, sweetly calling, "Mama?"

"I'll be right out. Just wait there for me." Swoosh, I sunk down into myself like a fast ride down a water slide until I could barely hear them, unconsciously arranging foam letters in the bathtub.

After a few minutes, Sarah called again, "Almost done, Mama?"

Her hopeful hesitation flattened me with shame. "Just another minute."

Mom called motherhood a vocation. I believe it was for her, but I never felt called to it. I walked into it with an open heart and mind, but struggled to find my place. Standing up, I looked at myself in the bathroom mirror. I grabbed a hair tie and pulled back my hair, splashed cold water on my face, and opened the door.

"Girls! There you are." They both giggled, taken by surprise. "Let's go outside." I scooped Amelia up. Sarah cheered and Amelia stuck her hand directly down my shirt and rested it on my breast. We stepped in and out of the maze of yarn in the kitchen to the back door.

That day, I got it together by building a fairy garden, where they diligently played on my birthday—the first day of summer, offering me a perfect hour of peace. With my face to the sun, I resisted the urge to read Deenie's diary or plan the meal I wanted to make later for Mom and Sadie.

Once the girls were sufficiently sun-kissed and dirty, I bathed and dressed them for my mom's impending arrival. She greeted me with a "happy birthday" as I opened the door holding a cup of green tea. I moved the hot mug out of the way so she could wrap her arms around me.

"Are my girls ready for a day at the zoo?"

I put the mug down and turned back to the juicy cantaloupe on my cutting board. "They are. Thanks for doing this, Mom. I'm really looking forward to having the afternoon to myself." The warm melon scent filled the kitchen as I packed it into a glass container and put it into the girls' bag.

Mom grabbed a stray piece of melon off of the cutting board. "Our afternoon snack? Lovely. Did you enjoy your morning? Did Jake do anything special?"

"He had to leave early today, but he's got something planned for later." I opened the window to my left. "I had a perfect morning. The girls kept themselves busy in the yard and I spent a full hour just sitting out there daydreaming."

"How many times I found you sitting up against that old maple tree in our yard staring at the sky. I'd be all over the house calling your name and sure enough, you'd be lying outside somewhere with those glossy eyes."

"I don't do it enough. I can't believe how recharged I feel," I answered. "Would you like a cup of coffee?" I pointed to the half-empty pot.

"No, no...I'm fully caffeinated. We should probably head out soon. What do you have planned for the afternoon?" She tucked her hair behind her ears. "You should take a long, lovely bath or get a massage or something."

"I'm making a picnic feast for us to share later when I meet you all back at Grandpa's."

She scrunched her nose. "You're going to squander your time alone cooking?"

I questioned my decision for a moment, but found

my resolve. "I'm going to revel in my quiet house and uninterrupted time in the kitchen. And we'll *all* benefit!"

"I just want to make sure you're doing something for yourself. It's your birthday." She smiled and walked into the living room. "Who wants to go see some monkeys?" She spun the girls around and they were ready to go and through the door, a chaotic parade of kisses, snacks and joyful anticipation.

Alone in the house, I stood in my kitchen absorbing the silence. Although things were on a positive trajectory with Jake, the long winter and spring drained me. A happy birthday meant taking time to nourish myself and not feel guilty about it, even if the nourishment came from sources my mom didn't recognize. She meant well, but she didn't get it. There was no overthinking with three pots on the stove. There was only smelling for singe, tasting before the boil, and watching for that perfect shade of green on the broccoli or asparagus. These simple actions were my radical response to every comment she made about me *being the glue*, as well as to everything I read or listened to or was told that I should want or want to be: a sacrificial mother, a perfect wife, or a woman with more important career goals. I wanted to start my next year, not as the woman I tried to be, but the woman I authentically was.

Whenever I felt overwhelmed, Sadie would ask me, "What is the next right step?"

The next right step was to feed this body that kept moving me through the world when it seemed impossible. I grabbed scissors out of the drawer next to the sink and walked across the kitchen and through the back door. In my bare feet, I walked across the warm fieldstones of our patio to the herbs growing tall in terra cotta pots. As I clipped the piney rosemary and the sweet basil, my mind swirled with ideas for my birthday feast. First, I needed to feed myself.

I dug my toes into the wooly thyme growing around the edges of the patio stones and thought about Deenie sifting soil through her hands to work through her sadness. For weeks I read about the beginnings of Deenie's garden in her diary. She transplanted some things from the woods but lost steam in the summer. By autumn, the entries were few and far between, but there was more to her story and certainly more to her garden. For my birthday, I would find a way to embody the parts of her that resonated within me.

I carried the bundles of herbs into the kitchen and washed the sticky sap of the rosemary from the tips of my thumb and fingers—the medicinal, earthy oils lingering in my nostrils. I walked from the kitchen to the dining room and upstairs, opening every window in the house. In my bedroom, as the curtains flew out and away from the window in the breeze, I took off my ripped t-shirt and paint-spotted shorts and pulled a long, gauzy sundress over my head. I pulled my thick curls into a bun and put on the big, copper, hoop earrings that Sadie brought back from Sedona. I rubbed lotion onto my face and hands, then grabbed the tangerine roller ball from my top drawer and rolled it along the inside of my wrists and behind my ears.

Downstairs, I crossed the threshold into the kitchen and the choir in my mind began the chant, at first nearly imperceptible but growing louder with my confidence. I lit the candle behind the sink, scattered among three plants: an aloe plant, a shamrock, and a Christmas cactus that bloomed white in December. A Black Madonna prayer card sat nestled into the corner of one window and a copper ornament hanging with one of Nana Wanda's crosses in the other. Below it was a small glass bowl of water with a red stone inside that an old friend brought me from a Caribbean beach. The only way to see the deep mulberry color of the stone was to keep it in water; on land it faded into a dusty rose.

Breathing in from the bottom of my belly, I exhaled slowly and released the anxiety about my life, like clearing myself as a vessel for the energy that I prayed would travel through me and into this meal. I poured the wine. Whiskey or beer was for a night around the fire pit or a reward at the end of a long week. I drank sacramental red wine in the kitchen.

I turned the music on. The sun streamed through the open windows onto the butcher block counter and the sound of the horns accompanying Sarah Vaughan's deep, velvet voice sent a pulsing energy from the bottoms of my feet to the swing of my hips. It filled my chest, down my arms, to my fingertips. I occupied my space with every movement and all of my senses.

I traced the florets of the cauliflower with my fingertips, grateful for my hands. I trusted my hands. They carried me through the meditation of chop, chop, chopping the cauliflower, tossing it with a steady stream of oil, and sprinkling pink salt and curry powder. The turmeric burst forth in a cloud from the bottle and dispersed into the air. I tasted the bitter, peppery orange cloud in my mouth and throat as I slid the cauliflower into the oven.

My hands worked from their own consciousness, dicing the onion, carrots, and garlic and caramelizing them together in olive oil. A slight singe alerted me to taste and the unctuous sweetness of the onions practically dissolved on my tongue. I pulled the nutty, orange-tinged cauliflower florets out of the oven and added them, along with a broth, to my pot. I pureed it with the swoosh and churn of my immersion blender, and in a cascade of brightness, I poured freshly squeezed lime juice into the pot and mixed. I followed that with a creamy, warm coconut milk that I dreamily stirred into spirals with my wooden spoon.

I grabbed a stray piece of roasted cauliflower and closed my eyes to taste the salty brown edges and deep, earthy curry. A freshly charged energy engaged my elbow and wrist while I stirred and my hips as they rolled to the music, with my legs and feet rooted as the wind picked up around me. Outside, I noticed the sky imbued with a strange yellow hue. Like the creamy, spicy soup in the pot below me, a storm began to bubble. Something in the breeze whispered in my ear that the fullness in my body and spirit meant that whatever came from my hands would be divine. The alchemy only happened whenever I surrendered the way I did that day.

In my quest to embody Deenie, I made a beautiful bisque. Swirling the milk around, I sang into the pot until the cream was devoured by the exquisite orange. I poured it into my favorite blue bowl, swallowed it bite by bite, and imagined it healing and transforming me from the inside. Happy birthday, Jess.

With my belly and heart full, I grabbed Deenie's diary and took it upstairs to my bedroom, as thunder boomed and echoed around me. Something shifted at that point in her story.

The writing didn't always make sense. There were long jumps in time when she didn't write. She wrote about my mom and later Sadie–when they started to laugh, or crawl, or Nana Wanda's love for them. After she wrote the long entry that culminated in the beginning of the garden, she barely mentioned it again, and she never mentioned Grandpa. She alluded to having a hard time occasionally but often just stopped writing mid-sentence on those days. I was hoping for more revelation at this point. With a dog at my feet, and the rain pounding against my bedroom window, I settled in to read.

Dear Diary, *June 20, 1961*

During the week, Paul comes back from the bar after I've gone to bed and spends most of the weekend there. I used to treasure my solitude but there is none of that in a life with two children. It was a lonely winter with no one but my mother for adult conversation. Even if there had been something to record, I didn't have the energy to write.

The spring provided some relief; I started focusing my attention on the garden. I feel different out there—in my body, everything connecting. It's coming along nicely, except for the roses. I planted them last fall in the full sun of the front yard and I'm not seeing a bud. Mrs. Carini doesn't know roses. She only knows vegetables.

On a day too beautiful to stay inside, I remembered the woman in the cigarette pants who mentioned her roses. I hadn't seen her in town after that day and decided to check for her again after Mumma took the girls to the knitting circle. Maybe she could give me some advice.

My muscles buzzed with energy as I climbed onto the bus and admired my reflection in the window. When I arrived, I saw her table across the street, surrounded by people. I waited for traffic to pass and as I stepped out into the street, I felt her eyes on me with the same intensity as the day we met. I smoothed my hair and opened the top button of my dress, willing my heart to slow down.

"You've returned. For the bracelet?" She spoke with an accent. How did I miss that before? Something that I couldn't place, but reminiscent of my grandmother.

I asked her if the bracelet had been sold.

She continued, "You left so quickly that day. I wasn't sure if I would see you again and I didn't even get to learn your name." She walked around the table with the copper acorn bracelet and approached me, opening it in the middle and looking down to place it on my wrist. "I'm Lillian." When she lifted her head, I could feel her breath on my face. Her brown eyes were luminous and warm. She smelled like books and lilacs and something else familiar that I couldn't name.

She'd kept the bracelet for me, hoping I'd return someday.

"Yes, the copper is beautiful with those striking blue eyes. The moment you stepped off of the bus, I saw the light around you. This bracelet belongs to you." She cupped my hands with hers and told me she couldn't charge me for something that was supposed to find its way to me. She invited me to a party at her home that weekend to celebrate the beginning of summer. Scooting back around the table, she retrieved a pen and a slip of paper from her purse.

She wrote her number and address on the back and handing it to me, she said, "Saturday. Come? Mother and I are just over the hill." She pointed toward the tracks on the other side of the market.

"Yes. We'll come." I smiled.

"You are a we?"

"My husband, Paul."

"Well, bring him." Her eyes met mine and held them a moment longer than felt comfortable. "I'd like to meet him."

My eyes drifted down to her red lips. Self-conscious, I said a quick goodbye and headed toward the market, realizing that I never told her my name. When I got onto the next bus, I pulled out the paper that she gave me—a department store receipt. I scanned the address she wrote to see where she lived then turned the receipt over to see what she bought.

Lipstick. Rouge Dior #9. DK

23. MIA

The girls and I drove through a quick storm on our way to the
zoo that washed the thick, sticky morning clean. Later that
afternoon, we left the monkeys to meet up with Sadie and Jess.

"What do those signs say, Grandma?" Sarah stared at eight
or ten striking workers outside of the oil refinery in The Bottoms.
I pulled the car over and explained what I could.

"Can we share our girl scout cookies with them?" She pointed
to the boxes stacked up on the passenger seat of my car.

I handed four boxes back to Sarah and she passed them, one
at a time, through the car window.

"She wanted to support your efforts," I said.

"That's a real Pittsburgh girl you got there," he answered.
"You're raising her right."

I smiled the rest of the way to Presston, thinking about his response. I liked the idea that respect for union culture was in our blood.

From the swing at Presston park, I watched Sarah and Amelia dig into the dirt under a metal slide. Dirty children are happy
children. Amelia picked rocks out of the dirt and Sarah smoothed
the holes left behind to even the ground out. It made me wonder
if Mama's love for the soil was in their blood too.

The swing jerked forward from a little push. I held on tighter
to the metal chains and glanced behind me as the swing slipped

backward to find Sadie's easy eyes and smiling, high cheekbones. She pushed harder the second time and I laughed loudly, giving in to the momentum.

Sadie joined me in laughing. "There it is: my favorite laugh, of all the laughs, in all the world." She sat down on the swing to my left as my own swing slowly drifted to a stop. "Mrs. Carini's granddaughter pulled out before I parked. It's nice that she visits so often."

"Isabella?" I asked. "Remember her as a little girl with all that dark, curly hair? Poor Jessie would beg me to invite her to play at our house, but you know Mrs. Carini."

Sadie waved to the girls as she spoke. "Isn't Isabella's little girl around Sarah's age? It's a shame they didn't come over here."

I pumped my legs. "All of the problems her boys caused in Presston and Mrs. Carini still thinks of us as the troubled ones."

"I ran into Tony Carini at Eat'n Park a few weeks ago. I think he's the manager there now. I hadn't seen him since Joey's funeral. He said Louie got assigned to a parish in Washington County."

"Father Louie," I corrected her.

Sadie laughed. "That still kills me. Father Louie who used to peek into our bedrooms while we changed clothes."

"Remember how close the Carini boys and the Williams boys used to be? They took such different paths after the factory closed. Ricky's a firefighter and Dave joined the Navy."

Sadie backed up and released her swing forward, legs straight out in front of her. "I loved growing up here but after Pressed Steel closed, it wasn't the same community. It wasn't the Presston I recognized: the horde of sweaty men walking home after the night shift or later at dinnertime..."

You could set your clock by them, on their way to the beer garden at the end of either shift.

Sadie continued, "Stada babas sweeping the sidewalk first thing in the morning, jukebox music from the beer garden on the weekend, sitting on the porch of the candy store after school with banana popsicles, and all the kids scattering when the streetlights started flickering on. I could depend on Presston. Why did they cut down all the sycamore trees? It was around that same time."

An unusual bird call distracted me from Sadie's words.

"At least it bounced back somewhat," she said.

"Has it?" I pointed out a Cooper's Hawk flying above us.

The large hawk cut through the air high above the playground and toward the woods. Sadie turned back to me, delighted at the sight and surprised that I could name it. I gave you the credit of course, Mark. You knew the name of every bird.

"I don't think I ever looked up before I met Mark," I told her. "I just kept my eyes on the ground directly in front of me. I've been trying to look up more."

The hawk soared back toward the park, striped in a warm brown, spotted underneath with chocolate raindrops.

"Remember when we would swing as high as we could here and have a contest to see who could kick their shoes the farthest?" I pumped my legs and Sadie joined in, trying to overtake me.

The girls turned around to see us and giggled as our shoes came flying toward them.

As Sadie's swing slowed down beside me, she said, "Sarah has your beautiful laugh, Mia. It's good to laugh with you more and remember the old days."

She got up and moved behind me to give another push, bracelets jingling, and she asked about Jess. I told her that I took the girls out so she could have some quiet time and she wasted the day cooking for us. On my right, I noticed Jess pulling in front of the house.

Sarah ran toward us with our shoes. Behind me, Sadie put her hands above mine on the chain link and slowed the swing to a stop. I leaned over to kiss Sarah on the top of her head and thanked her, slipping my shoes back on.

"I'll corral the girls. You go help her with those bags." Sadie put her shoes on and took Sarah by the hand to walk back toward Amelia. I made my way toward the gray house and Jess turned around from the door to walk back to the car, just in time to see me.

24. JESS

The breeze that blew through Presston had been steamed, rinsed, then baked warm by the afternoon sun. I laid the food out on a blanket in the garden: baskets of homemade pita bread wrapped up in red and orange cotton napkins, little purple bowls of different flavors of hummus, bigger orange bowls of vegetables, and a very colorful tabbouleh salad. Next to the salad, I placed a lime green mug full of sprouts, a bright yellow mixing bowl full of strawberries, and a white casserole full of roasted eggplant with walnuts and parsley.

"Jessie, all your favorites—gorgeous. Is Jake at work?" Sadie asked with a cautious tone and hopeful eyebrows.

"He is." I smiled at her, going from Sarah to Amelia with a wet washcloth. "We have plans this evening."

Sadie helped Sarah fill her plate, following her finger as she pointed at everything she wanted to eat.

Mom patted the ground beside her. "Sit with me, Jessie. You've spent your whole birthday cooking. It's time you relaxed."

I tried to convince her that I couldn't be more relaxed. "I made a promise to Sadie to spend less time worrying about checking off all of the wife and mother boxes and more time doing things that make me feel like me. Cooking makes me feel like me."

Seeing her sister's confused expression, Sadie jumped in. "What a good lesson for her daughters." She turned to me, asking, "Isn't that what you want for them?"

I nodded. "It is. I'm letting things go."

Mom looked lost. "Letting things go? What are you letting go? And Sadie, how are you an authority on being a wife and mother?"

Sadie forced a smile. "I never claimed to be."

Mom took a deep breath. "I can't understand how making your loved ones the priority could be wrong? We have to take care of each other. You can't *let go* of that."

Sarah pushed herself onto her Mom's lap, knocking a piece of pita off of her plate.

I picked it up and handed it to Mom like a peace offering. "I'm anxious–following your map. I'm making my own map." I gently touched her knee. "It doesn't mean that yours is wrong."

Mom put her hand on mine. "You know, I haven't seen you so calm and easy in some time." She kissed the top of Sarah's head, keeping her eyes down. "I'm sorry for being defensive, girls. I'm working on it."

Sarah and Amelia got antsy after dinner so Sadie went up into the attic and brought down a box of old toys. Back outside, in front of the girls, she reached down into the box and put her fingers around a small purple crocheted ball. As she lifted her arm, we realized that the ball was the foot of a doll. Sarah and Amelia squealed and reached for it at the same time.

Mom's eyes filled with a wave of nostalgia. She quickly dropped her eyes to the right of her leg just off the blanket and started pulling a couple of dandelion greens that had poked through the grass since our last visit. I put my hand on her knee again and asked if she was okay.

"Oh goodness yes, I don't know why I'm so emotional these days." Changing the subject, she said, "It's such a satisfying feeling to pull these out by the roots. Don't you think?"

Sadie told the girls that a very long time ago, Nana Wanda made the doll for Mom.

Sarah handed Mom the doll reverently and asked, "This is *your* baby?"

Mom made her voice sound more serious, to match Sarah's expression, and told her the doll's name. "Priscilla could probably use a washing, but you can take her home."

The girls oohed and ahhed over the purple crocheted skirt and the plastic head with crocheted purple hat. Mom's eyes filled again, seeing her granddaughters with the doll.

Sadie noticed and stepped in. "Just as my Mama made magic in this garden and your Mama made magic in the kitchen today, our Nana made magic this way. Everywhere she went, she carried around a basket of color and magical wands."

"I loved the sound of those clicking needles." Mom closed her eyes like she was trying to hear them in her mind.

Sadie, the storyteller, continued talking to the girls. "Soft woolen families of brown and white bunnies and beautiful princesses like Priscilla, layered in cotton candy pinks and purples, all started off as balls of yarn. Nana Wanda brought them to life."

Amelia ran her tiny fingers through the yellow yarn hair while Sarah picked white clover flowers and watched Sadie make a crown for the doll by weaving them together.

Mom said, "I can close my eyes and see that yarn on Nana Wanda's needles and now here it is, in between my granddaughter's fingers." She looked up anxiously at Sadie, like she needed to be rescued from her own emotions.

Sadie obliged, pulling Amelia up into her lap. "Let me tell you about Nana Wanda. She didn't hug and kiss like your grandma. Her love was warm, milky, sweet tea on rainy afternoons and the way her squishy arms jiggled when she laughed, watching us run through the laundry that she hung on a line in the sunshine."

Mom found her voice. "She stood behind us as we rolled out the noodles for her chicken noodle soup and spent hours gliding back and forth on the front porch with us..."

Sadie smiled at her knowingly, "smoking her Raleigh Plain End cigarettes, watching us play with all the creatures that came from her knitting basket."

Someone started a lawn mower as the smell of charcoal wafted through our picnic.

"Remember that brown blanket, Mia?" Sadie asked. "Nana Wanda knit big blocks of chocolate and caramel brown together and when I wrapped it around my shoulders, I could smell her on the yarn."

"*Cashmere Bouquet*," Mom remembered. "She always smelled like that soap."

"And clove gum," Sadie said.

I leaned toward the doll, hoping to catch the scent, but I only caught the stale smell of the attic.

Mom continued, "In the winter, we'd sit on the heat register and drape that brown blanket over us, so the hot air stayed under the blanket."

Sadie nodded, her arms around Amelia. "I could see the love that she knit into each individual stitch. I wondered what she thought about when she wrapped the yarn around, where she sat when she slipped it off the needle, how she worked her spells into every row."

Mom's eyes opened wide. "The knitting circle! My favorite was Mrs. Kosmatka who only wore black with nude nylons, even on a day like today. She made the best kolaczki cookies with apricot jam." She smiled at me. "They taught us to bake and knit and everything we brought home from the circle smelled like cigarettes and coffee."

I started stacking empty dishes on the blanket and asked Sadie if she remembered the knitting circle.

She nodded. "They were intimidating in a pack, but generous. One ball of yarn at a time, they did what women have done for ages: shared their joys and regrets as they knit and purled yarn into their celebrations and their sorrows."

I smiled at Mom, feeling her struggle with Sadie's dramatics. "Maybe you should get those needles out again, Mom, and work on your legacy."

She stood up to carry dishes into the kitchen. "Maybe I should make something for your birthday."

"Maybe you should make something for yourself," I answered.

"Speaking of your birthday, Jessie," Sadie interrupted, "I have something special planned for you. I met an intuitive at a friend's party last week. She's going to come over and read your tarot cards. Look at your schedule and let's pick an evening for the three of us to join her."

Mom glanced back from the door. "Oh, I don't know about that, girls, maybe you should do that one without me."

"Absolutely not. We're doing it together." Sadie yelled back.

Mom continued inside and came back out with sparkling lemonade. We toasted my birthday while the girls picked a rainbow of zinnias and Sadie made crowns for them to match Priscilla's.

25. MIA

I told you, Mark. Didn't I say Sadie would try to get me to a seance? She claimed it was a tarot card reading for Jess, but I know she's up to something. Nana Wanda said those cards opened a door for the devil. That's what she told Mama when she found out that Lillian brought them to our house.

"Calling personal power and independent thought *the devil* keeps the masses in line," Sadie said. "The cards give me clarity and validate things I already know."

She assured me that she organized a bit of fun, but I drove home from Jess's birthday dinner feeling guilty anyway. Approaching St. Philip's, I noticed the full parking lot. What would Nana Wanda think of my lazy faith? I instinctively pulled into the lot and parked my car in the last available space. I remembered the peaceful smile on her face as she prayed the rosary under her breath. With her favorite hymn in my ear, I wanted to feel close to her.

Humming *It is Well with My Soul*, I ran up the cement steps and into the familiar sanctuary. As a young girl, I used to sit in the dark sanctuary of St. Mary's while the choir practiced in the loft above. God was the consistent parent I craved. He listened to my fears and comforted me with the right hymn at mass or a reading that answered my questions.

All of my friends were Catholic. Mass was a social event and we tried to sit in the line of sight of the person we had a crush on. We waited all year for the summer lawn fete where we enjoyed a particular kind of freedom: late-night, church-sanctioned revelry that sounded like accordion music and smelled like cabbage and fried dough. For one long weekend, they lit the church parking lot like a carnival and the kids were permitted to be outside after the streetlights came on. The parents gambled and drank with Father Walt while we played all the festival games and danced a polka with the old folks. In high school, everyone wanted a gold St. Christopher medal as much as they wanted bell bottoms. Nana Wanda bought me one for my last birthday before she died. Being Catholic wasn't just our religion, it was our culture.

Approaching the back row of pews, I slid in and tried to remember the last time I went to Mass. Recently, when I arrived searching for that validating hymn or reading, I left disappointed. I tried to bring Sarah and Amelia as often as I could, but they distracted me. On the holidays, we stood in the back of the crowded church and I couldn't hear well.

I eased the kneeler down to avoid interrupting the standing congregation around me. With the burning incense and candles in my nose, I kneeled and hung my head. I rested my face on my folded hands and released the tension in my neck, but distractions intruded on every attempt to pray for Nana Wanda.

"You better pray for me when I'm gone, Mia," she said, before reminding me that my prayers might keep her out of purgatory.

It would make Mama happy to see us all together in her garden. I prayed for God to take away the fear in my throat when I thought about Sadie or Jess being like Mama. Feeling it worsen, I stood with the people around me, shoulders back, to open up my chest and lungs. I breathed in as deeply as I could and concentrated on the priest, vibrant in his vestments, with a multiplicity of colors behind him in the floor to ceiling stained glass. Preoccupied with a couple chatting at the far end of the pew, I realized that I wasn't going to get what I came there to find. I pulled my shirt down at my hips and adjusted the scarf keeping my short gray curls out of my face. I reached down and pulled the tongue of my tennis shoe out. Behind the chatting couple, I noticed the heavy iron radiators against the wall as sweat crawled down between my shoulder blades.

I didn't recognize that church anymore or the people in it. I barely believed but relied on the possibility. The church was like a different kind of grandmother who nursed my skinned knees, but I stopped visiting once I grew up. I pulled back because it became harder to overlook her eccentricities. She wasn't everything she claimed to be and didn't put up a fight when I stopped visiting, so my visits became briefer and farther between. On the holidays, I was too busy with my own grandchildren to pay attention to her, and now she's gone. Grief flooded my insides until there was no space left to fill my lungs.

I kicked the kneeler back up with one foot and hurried out, knocking into the card table in the lobby holding the plastic rosaries that the nuns made. Back in my car, I worried for a moment that I might be having a heart attack. How foolish to be my age and so unsure about everything. As a young woman, I moved with confidence. Nana was steady and Mama was chaos. I chose the safe path and did everything right. Now, in my fifties, I couldn't say with any certainty that I did *anything* right. Jessie seemed constantly conflicted, while Sadie floated through life. I turned the ignition and started driving.

I felt better as soon as my car approached the oak trees. At home, I went deep into the closet and yanked a box down from the top shelf. Opening it, I found Nana's favorite knitting needles and a bag of yarn that I purchased years ago to make a baby blanket for Sarah. Sadie said something about Nana Wanda knitting and purling energy into our blanket. One by one, I pulled the skeins of yarn out: fiery reds, thick woolen blood reds, and thin cotton pink and violet sunsets. Together those colors captured something of summer that I could wrap around my shoulders in the autumn. I didn't need to figure out a life path, only the next step. I would stitch them together, not to hold a baby, but to hold myself.

26. JESS

After my birthday dinner with Mom and Sadie, I found Jake on our front stoop waiting with a bouquet of sunflowers.

"Happy Birthday Jess." He kissed me. "Come on. Let's go."

"Go where?"

"Girls, who wants to go exploring? Sarah, put on your rain boots." He picked Amelia up and opened the hall closet to get the backpack carrier that she sat in for hikes.

Confused, but carried along by his energy, I remembered this was the man I fell in love with. I went into the kitchen and started packing snacks.

"What do we need?" I yelled from the kitchen.

"Nothing. Just get some boots on and meet me out front."

Sarah bustled with excitement, sensitive to the energy change in the house. We stepped through the front door and looked down the street a bit to see Jake pointing up at the steps and talking to Amelia, who sat in a pack on his back and played with his hair. We caught up to them quickly.

Our neighborhood, The Slopes, was a community of hillside dwellers overlooking downtown Pittsburgh. An enormous Roman Catholic church sat on one corner of our narrow street with a bar on the opposite corner. A few doors down from our house there were two sets of steps to go up or down the hill by

The Mission Market. People traveled from all over the city for their kielbasa at Christmas.

In the height of the industrial boom, that great hill was home to many of the German, Irish, and Eastern European immigrants who worked in the steel mill, down by the river in The Flats. The history of the people who helped build the city survived in the geography and the buildings, but at the bottom of the steps, in The Flats, a person was exposed to some of the city's culture and considerable local pride. During football season, cheers (or groans) filled the sidewalks from all the bars and everyone wore black and gold. During Lent, there were fish frys and pierogi sales at all of the old churches. On St. Patrick's weekend, revelers started in the morning at the parade downtown—one of the biggest in the country. Afterward, they walked across the bridge, over the river, to the bars in The Flats. In October, people dressed up as zombies and limped around the streets in honor of *The Night of the Living Dead*, filmed in Pittsburgh by one of our own—something I discovered after being surrounded by zombies near the doorway of my favorite coffee shop.

Not knowing the plan typically made me uneasy, but that night, I felt exhilarated by the loss of control. I grabbed Sarah's hand and we followed Jake up the *sky park steps* that climbed high above our house and ended at the unnamed playground near the top that Sarah named *sky park*. The Slopes were meant to be traversed on foot. The streets were too narrow for more than one car to pass by at a time, though drivers were patient and friendly about pulling over and taking turns. The best way for a pedestrian to navigate the whole neighborhood was on the sixty-eight different sets of steps called *paper streets*—labeled and named like other streets on a map of Pittsburgh. These public stairways climbed up the steep hillside and cut across it, zigging and zagging up and down the hill throughout the entire neighborhood.

Weeds shot up through the spaces between the cement steps and reached from the sides, tickling Sarah's legs. Even though you could see downtown Pittsburgh across the river, some of the houses were secluded and hidden in the trees, only accessible on foot from those steps. Halfway up the steps, we peeked through a break in the railing at an overgrown path to a decrepit home sitting back in the woods. We stopped, wondering if it was deserted but deciding that it wasn't. There were potted ferns on the porch next to a rusted metal chair and Sarah noticed a freshly painted, red and white-spotted cement mushroom by the tree closest to the house. We continued up the next set of steps imagining who might live there.

I began. "I think it's a witch. And she is too busy conjuring wonders to leave her house."

Jake leaned down. "Maybe it's a very old man who once worked down in the steel mill and walked up all of these steps after work every day with groceries from the Mission Market for his wife. I bet they sat on that porch after dinner while their ten children played and hung from the trees."

"Ma, ma, maybe it's a dog!" Sarah squealed. "And he keeps the door open for all the dogs who get lost and need a place to sleep when it gets cold outside."

We passed the sky park and continued up the steps to the next street, out of breath from laughing and climbing. Jake pointed toward the west where we could see the sun starting to dip down toward the horizon.

"See that patch of woods? That's where we're headed."

Instead of tall, narrow city houses like ours, the houses higher up were wider, almost suburban houses with grassy yards and trees. Further down the street, when we got to another patch of woods, we swapped kids. I took Amelia in the carrier and Jake took Sarah's hand. With Amelia's hands in my hair, we walked through the woods and found more remnants of old houses tucked away and more city stairs leading farther and farther up the great hill. Sarah picked up every interesting stone and dragged her hand across every mossy tree, so I walked slowly with the girls while Jake moved ahead. He found an oak with low branches and climbed up, grabbed onto a vine, and after a strong enough yank, swung out and down to the girls' amazement as I resisted the urge to stop him. It took me back to a night before we were married. We hiked all day and swung out on a vine into a swimming hole, found the perfect spot to camp, and spent the night naked in the woods.

As the light faded, the cicadas' song swelled around us and I noticed the full moon rising, just like the night Jake and I spent alone in the woods. After the girls were born, spontaneity became liability. Jake's wild embrace of life, that I once admired, started to feel like impetuous choices. He beamed as the girls cheered for him and I felt sorry for the pressure I put on him. For a moment, I even felt sorry for the pressure I put on myself.

"Come on, follow me down here." Jake pointed to my left. "There's a little path if you don't want to swing over." He headed back toward us on the path and reached out for Sarah's hand. Keeping his eyes on me, his expression told me that he remembered our camping trip as well.

We hiked deeper into the woods to a clearing with the final surprise: a cloud of lightning bugs hovering near a wide, shallow puddle at the bottom of a tiny hillside spring. We got Amelia out of the carrier and Sarah sweetly caught one for her sister. Watching their solemn faces as it slowly walked up Amelia's arm, opened its wings and flew off, I reached for his hand, which he squeezed and kissed.

I wiped a tear from his cheek and kissed his lips. He leaned his forehead down against mine and we stood there for a few minutes, eyes closed, breathing, and listening to our daughters speak to fireflies.

We ambled out of the woods in the moonlight and walked back down the steps in grateful silence. Amelia nearly fell asleep in the pack on Jake's back, while he carried Sarah down the last set of steps.

When we got to the house, I whispered, "I don't want to go in yet, it's such a beautiful night." We sat on our front stoop and Sarah sleepily pointed to the bubbles by the door, next to the sidewalk chalk.

"I don't know if we can see the bubbles in the dark? What do you think?" I asked Jake.

"I think we have to try? I don't think I've ever blown bubbles at night," he answered, passing Sarah to me.

He picked up the blue plastic container and walked down the two steps of the stoop onto the sidewalk.

"Ready?" he asked Sarah, and she nodded her head quickly in anticipation.

He lifted the plastic bubble wand to his lips, took a slow, deep inhale, and as he blew through the hole in the wand, a steady stream of flickering lights appeared and floated around us. Instead of bubbles, we saw the reflection of the street light on the side of them.

"Fairies! Daddy made fairies." Sarah hopped off of my lap and turned around, wide-eyed and encircled by floating lights. She climbed down off of the stoop to join Jake on the sidewalk.

Amelia woke up and I pulled her out of the pack so she could join her sister. Jake squatted down to Sarah's level, brought the wand to his lips, and blew a stream of tiny lights toward the sky.

When we finished, Jake offered to put the girls to bed. I walked them upstairs, grabbed a bottle of wine and a glass, and went back out to the stoop. It seemed surprisingly quiet for a summer evening in our city neighborhood. I gazed ahead at the lights of the tall university cathedral east of the city and the passing cars on the freeway far ahead. Jake appeared in no time.

"That was fast. Sleepy girls?"

"Bring your wine to the back yard. One more surprise," he said and waved from the door.

We walked through the house to the back door and I spotted a round cake, topped with familiar flowers, on the small plastic table between our two chairs.

"Are these from?" I started to ask.

"Deenie's garden," he answered. "I stopped by on my way to work this morning. I'm sorry, Jess. I know that place is important. I never should have said those things."

My eyes burned and all of the tenderness of the evening streamed out. "I'm ashamed of the way I've treated you. I let my fears change the way I saw you. I know I've made you feel bad about who you are." I laughed through tears, thinking of our family time in the woods. "And I love who you are!" A dog barked from far away as I tried to contain my fluctuating emotions. "Are we growing apart?"

He put his hand on the side of my face, wiping a tear with his thumb. "I don't think we're growing apart. I think that life is thrusting things onto us and forcing us to change. That's not necessarily bad. We can fix this." His voice broke. He took a shaky breath and held my hand in both of his. "*I* feel ashamed. The way that you accept my attempts to be better, the way that you're looking at me right now, even after the things that I've..." A momentary look of guilt crossed Jake's face but he quickly rearranged his expression into an easy smile. "We'll figure it out, but not tonight. Tonight, let's just be together out here like the night we went camping, remember? Before the girls?"

"I do."

"Let's just be Jess and Jake tonight, out in the woods, with wine and cake."

We stayed out there for hours, laughing and talking, and I fell asleep more hopeful than I'd been in a long time. At three in the morning, I woke up thinking about Deenie, so I skipped my nightly visit to confirm the girls were still breathing and snuck downstairs for a cup of tea and another diary entry.

Dear Diary,   *June 25, 1961*
On the evening of Lillian's party, I walked to the car through the heavy night air, thick with the sweet scent of honeysuckle growing on the edge of the woods. I peeled my dress from the small of my back and caught a glimpse of my hair, swollen like the clouds that followed us on the dark drive. About 10 minutes outside of Presston, we pulled onto her street and passed a woman trying to comfort a wailing baby on the porch of a dilapidated house, then a man having a coughing fit outside of a corner store. As our car approached the house, I knew that the purple door had to be Lillian's. When she opened it to welcome us, we were greeted with an explosion of color and the smell of oranges. The kinds of things that she might sell at her table in town lined every surface and hung on all the walls.

She only looked at me. "Welcome, beautiful blue eyes."

"That's my Blue Gardenia." Paul smiled. "I'm Paul, thanks for having us." He stepped in front of me and extended his hand to Lillian.

When he walked through to the next room, I grabbed her hand. "Deenie. My name is Deenie."

She kissed my cheek hello, held her cheek close to mine for five extra seconds and I breathed her in: turpentine.

"Deenie is short for?" she asked, her red lips near my ear.

I looked down and smiled. "Geraldine." I took another deep breath in. Yes, definitely turpentine—the smell I couldn't name before.

"You paint?" I noticed an oil painting just beyond the curve of her neck. I recognized her mother in the painting from our first meeting and marveled at the rich colors and thick textures that danced out from behind Lillian's face in front of me.

"Yes." She stepped to the side of me to face the painting. "I did that one with palette knives. I tried to capture mother the way I remember her, when she was younger and full of life." She turned back to me. "I spend all of my money on plants, paints, and lipstick." She laughed a long, lovely, melodious laugh and the whole house seemed to erupt into laughter with her.

Paul and Lillian hit it off immediately. Watching the two of them together, it struck me that they had a very similar way of carrying themselves. Lillian introduced him to an artist friend who also served in Korea, and he and Paul sat together at the kitchen table for hours. After the party thinned out, Lillian and I stayed in the back yard, as the clouds moved on and the humidity surrendered to dew drops on the grass below us. We took our shoes off and planted our feet, staring in a comfortable silence at the trembling stars. Then we talked for hours, drinking whiskey and eating raspberries. The air, the drinks, and her curiosity left me intoxicated and reacquainted with parts of myself that seemed lost since I had the girls. DK

27. MIA

Do you see those storm clouds, Mark? Jess and I finished transplanting a few things yesterday; now they'll get a good soaking. I got a postcard from Sadie this morning.

> July 5, 2009
> Dear Mia, The redwoods are transformative. It's
> humbling to stand before something ancient.
> Remembering the way Mama described her
> honeymoon trip makes me want to see all the
> things that she didn't get to see. That's a lesson
> I learned from her, to experience it all while we
> can because tomorrow isn't promised. Makes it all
> more meaningful, imagining her living through
> us. I'd love to show you someday. Love, Sadie

She sounded happy but I felt sad reading that.

It's good to be out here with you. I haven't seen you as much lately, but you'd never miss watching the dark clouds roll in from the west. I love that our porch sits so high that we can see the horizon miles and miles away. We've had so many beautiful sunsets from this spot and watched so many storm clouds roll in.

Yesterday, little Sarah smelled the pink roses by the porch and Jess told her about the first time that you bought her roses like that for Valentine's Day. When she wants to calm me down, she starts talking about you. Apparently Sadie had been talking to Jess about our parents like they were some kind of great love story. I concentrated on the task in front of me and hummed a song but Jess knows when I'm upset. Great love story? I'll tell you about this great love story.

One day, Mama got dressed up and gathered the money she'd stashed around the house that Daddy didn't know about. You remember those two steps that lifted up, where she used to hide money? She hid money in an envelope under the couch cushion because Daddy only sat in the recliner, and all of the coins she found went into the metal box at the bottom of her underwear drawer.

I don't think she'd slept in days. She ran around the house in a pink suit with a matching hat that I'd only ever seen hanging in her closet. She put Sadie and me in the dresses we wore to church with Nana and we walked through our back yard to the alley behind us, and down toward the bus stop. I assume we took the long way to avoid passing the front of Nana's house.

On the bus, Mama talked to everyone: the old man with a tiny red feather in his gray felt hat and the lady who smelled like she didn't take baths. My stomach hurt when Mama talked so much. We passed our normal stop and rode on to downtown Pittsburgh. I tugged on her dress and asked where we were going.

Mama's eyes and smile were wider than usual. "We're going to Kaufmann's. I have a big day planned for us. We're going to have lunch and go to the movies and do some very special shopping."

We went straight to the giant department store for French onion soup in the Tic Toc restaurant and after we finished, Mama let us get treats from the Arcade Bakery. Then she took us to the top floor and bought a beautiful crystal vase. She held it in the sunlight shining in through the window and it made a hundred tiny rainbows on the floor. For a moment, I forgot the sinking feeling in my stomach.

Somehow it went from day to night while we were in the movie theater and the sinking feeling returned when Mama opened the theater door to darkness. We'd been gone too long. On the bus ride home, Mama made friends with a woman who had more shopping bags than she could carry. I held Sadie's hand and stared through the window at the moonlight floating on the river. The bus eventually drove through The Bottoms, where the onion domes of the Orthodox church glittered in the dark like beacons calling us home. Instead of signaling relief in my bones, they inspired dread. Shame bubbled in my belly.

Daddy met us at the door when we got back.

"I called your mother. I didn't know where you took the girls." He spoke to Mama with such urgency.

"You're drunk!" she yelled back. Mama proudly took her new vase out of the box and put it on the end table in front of the window that faced the sidewalk. "Look girls, now we have a special place to put the flowers we grow."

Already angry about us coming home late, when he saw what Mama bought, he lost it. They yelled back and forth at each other while Sadie and I sat together on the couch, still in our jackets and patent leather Mary Jane shoes. He picked up Mama's vase and threw it across the room. It shattered into a million pieces—a hundred rainbows lost.

Mama laughed maniacally. Daddy turned around to see Nana Wanda come through the front door and he passed her without a word and walked down the street toward the beer garden. Mama walked right over the broken glass and out to her garden.

Nana scanned the room then glared at me. "Mia, you and I have talked about this. Your Mumma isn't feeling well. Why didn't you tell her to bring you home when it got late? You could have called me. You know my phone number. You could have called collect. I showed you how to do that, Mia."

Nana grabbed the broom from the kitchen and swept up the broken glass. "Keep Sadie on the couch. You girls sit on that couch and don't move. I don't want you cutting your feet on this." She frantically swept glass into a dustpan as her voice got louder and louder.

"You should have called me when they started fighting. Do you know what could have happened if I hadn't come in just then?" She swept with sharp, angry arms. "Your Mumma is not well and you have to help her in those times and think about Sadie too. She's too little. Your Mumma isn't well."

She swept and yelled and eventually got quiet. Sadie and I sat silently on the couch. Nana went into the other room and blew her nose then got us ready for bed.

That night, I laid awake in bed hoping that Mama would come in and tell me that it was all just a big misunderstanding, but she never did. Compared to some of the other stuff, you wouldn't imagine that particular fight would leave much of an impression. I didn't know what might have happened if Nana Wanda hadn't come, but the possibilities tormented me after she said it. I should have done this or that thing and if I had, Daddy wouldn't have been so angry when we got back. Mama wouldn't have lost her beautiful vase that filled the room with a hundred tiny rainbows and spent the next two weeks in bed.

It makes me wonder, if I met Mama, independent of Nana Wanda's fears and expectations, would I admire her the way that Sadie does? Hell, if I met myself, independent of my own expectations of a mother or a sister, what would I think?

I'll tell you: I wouldn't even know myself.

28. JESS

I woke up early on the day we planned to meet the intuitive lady. Grateful that Jake planned to keep the girls for the afternoon, I tiptoed out with the diary so he could sleep in. From the door of the girls' bedroom, I found them snuggled together looking at the pictures in a book we read so many times that they memorized the story.

I squeezed in next to them. "Is it okay if I read my book while you read yours?"

They both smiled and nodded before looking back down at *Little Bear*, and I opened to the next entry in Grandma Deenie's diary.

Dear Diary,   *August 21, 1961*

As the summer goes on, I find that the more time that I spend with Lillian, the more I need to know about her and the more I want to share. I want to see her baby pictures and hear about the first time that she fell in love. Unable to keep her contained inside of my head, I catch myself talking about her to anyone that will listen. Paul is happy that I've found a friend, but Mumma looks suspicious.

Lillian and I talk every day. She brings flowers from her garden: exquisite bouquets of every different color, texture, and scent.

She leaves them at my back door to surprise me. I copy "Her breast is fit for pearls" by Emily Dickinson and send it to her address. I send a poem every week.

Whenever we're together, I make excuses to stand close. I brush her hair away from her eyes or let her wipe the stray eyelash from my cheek. Some nights, I sneak off to her place after everyone's asleep to listen to music in her back yard. Last night, on an especially hot evening, she showed up in my garden after the girls were in bed with a chilled bottle of white wine.

She walked around the garden, humming a song from the radio, and talked to me about flowers. "You have to plant hellebore. That would be perfect here. It'll be the first to bloom and greet you when we emerge from the winter."

I liked the way it sounded when she talked about us in the future. Making plans felt like a promise.

Lillian danced around the area swinging her arms, a stream of wine flowing out of her glass onto the ground, singing her lovely song when she abruptly stopped.

"Deenie, we have an audience," she whispered.

I looked up at the girls' window and didn't see anything when I realized that she meant Mrs. Carini next door. "Oh, ignore her. She's just a nebby neighbor."

"She's hanging something red in the window?" Lillian squinted and leaned forward. "What is that? A horn?" Then she started laughing a mischievous laugh. "Oh Deenie, she's warding off the evil eye."

I stood up and wrapped my arms around Lillian's side. Everything about being with her felt right, especially if Mrs. Carini thought it was wrong. DK

I closed the book and held it to my chest, letting Deenie's words sink in and settle. Mom made Lillian sound unimportant, but Deenie wrote like a woman falling in love.

The girls wanted breakfast, so I put my daydreams away and spent the morning with them. We ate at the dining room table next to an art project. I cut strips of fabric with different prints and colors and the girls glued them to a big poster board in a beautifully chaotic mosaic. The time flew by and the sound of the shower upstairs reminded me of my plans with Mom and Sadie. When Jake came down, we swapped places and I drove to Mom's, excited about the tarot reading and energized by my morning with the girls.

As I approached Mom's front door, I could hear the familiar back and forth between her and Sadie inside.

"I'm just saying Sadie, I feel funny having this woman in my home." Mom looked up and through the screen door. "There's Jess."

"Good, someone who will help you see sense," Sadie answered.

We all kissed hello and Sadie grabbed my hand. "Your gift is downstairs."

I laughed. "Mom, you put our intuitive friend in the basement?"

"I asked the psychic to wait at the card table in the game room. Nana's rolling in her grave. I can't believe I let *yinz* talk me into this."

Sadie put her arm around me. "I think your mother has a secret that she's afraid will come out."

We walked through the foyer, with its elaborate Victorian wallpaper and exquisite woodwork, through the homey, but perfectly organized and spotlessly clean kitchen, and around the bend to the left to reach the basement stairs. Even though they finished the basement fifteen years earlier, I caught a hint of that familiar mildew scent when I hit the first step. One by one, we took the creaky stairs down below the house, toward Mark's old man cave that he called *The Hermit Cave*. After Mark died, Mom used the space to play cards with her friends. Later, it became a playroom for my girls.

An older woman sat at the card table by the fireplace, drinking a cup of tea out of a yellow mug. She had no colorful bag or flowing skirt or amethyst necklace. Evelyn, the intuitive, reminded me of a warmer version of Mrs. Carini. She might've been in her late-sixties, with short gray hair and unruly eyebrows that framed her big brown eyes. She wore plastic clip-on earrings in the shape of melon-colored flowers, a button-down blouse in a plaid print, brown polyester pants with an elastic waist, and beige orthopedic shoes. She smiled the most beautiful smile— her mouth taking up half of her face, and immediately put me at ease.

We sat down with her and chatted for a few moments when Evelyn interrupted my mom.

"Ladies, I know that I'm here to give Jessica a reading but I'm feeling a lot of energy around Mia, and I'd like to go with that for now if you don't mind."

Mom, with hands folded on the table, started scratching the back of one thumb with the other and said nothing.

I spoke up, "Absolutely Evelyn, please feel free to go with whatever feels right."

Evelyn closed her eyes and slowed her breathing. We sat in silence for a few minutes as mom fidgeted.

"You carry a heavy burden, Mia," Evelyn said.

Mom continued rubbing her thumbs against each other and laughed. "Yes and everyone loves to tease me about it. I want to take care of everyone. I'm always worrying about these girls." Mom pointed at the yellow mug. "You're out of tea, Evelyn, can I run upstairs and grab the pot for you?"

"Thank you. I'm fine." Evelyn grabbed a black, vinyl purse from the floor beside her. "Perhaps we can start with the cards. Would you be comfortable with that, Mia?"

Mom turned her head and coughed into her elbow. "This is supposed to be for Jessie. I don't think that you need to bother with me."

Sadie put her hand on Mom's. "Come on Mia, let's see what the cards have to say. It's something new. You promised to try new things with me this year, remember?"

Mom nodded her head. Evelyn reached into her bag and retrieved a stack of large cards wrapped in a red silk scarf with a long, clear crystal pointed on both ends. She asked Mom to shuffle the cards and bring her attention to anything she might like clarity on. Mom quickly shuffled and cut the deck as instructed, practically throwing the cards back to her, before looking over at the last supper painting that Nana Wanda left her.

"Please choose three cards, Mia." Evelyn spoke softly. Mom did as instructed.

Evelyn raised her eyebrows, "Ah, two major arcana. Spirit is telling you to listen up."

29. MIA

The psychic looked at me with such affection. It reminded me of Nana Wanda, which wrapped me in comfort, then spun me in circles. My eyes landed on the painting Nana Wanda left me hanging above the couch. She found solace in surrounding herself with reminders of her faith. She placed Blessed Mother statues in every room and a framed photograph of Pope Paul VI hung by her telephone chair, but the velvety, brightly painted version of the Last Supper was her favorite treasure. What would she think if she saw me shuffling tarot cards? Evelyn explained something about how it all worked, but my eyes and thoughts were fixated on that painting.

She pointed to the first card, which represented me: The Hermit. Jess and Sadie both laughed, probably because we were in your *hermit cave*, Mark, but maybe because of the way that Sadie harassed me to get out more.

Evelyn said something about going within and traveling down into the cave of my innermost being. She kept talking but I was distracted by "innermost being." Nana would never say words like that. If I met this Evelyn at Walmart or something, which is where I could picture seeing her, I couldn't imagine that she would be talking about my innermost being either.

She continued, "You feel alone, but you aren't without support." She pointed to the lantern on the card, that would light the path and guide me back out of the darkness. "Do you know what or who might act as your lantern?"

I stumbled, saying something about knowing that I needed to change. She pointed to the second card: Judgment. It exerted some influence over the situation. I didn't like the look of that card: angels calling people from the grave like the last judgment Nana Wanda talked about.

Evelyn seemed to notice the concern on my face and told me that Judgment went well with The Hermit, who asked me to be introspective.

She said, "This card is asking you, while you are taking an account, to consider *your* responsibility in the situation. Are there things that you need to let go of? Have you considered yourself a victim, when in fact, you hold some responsibility?"

She told me that acknowledging my responsibility would help me to move forward. Evelyn kept talking but the beating in my ears continued to build and it became more difficult to focus on her words. She looked to me for some kind of acknowledgement and I scrambled, saying something about being a martyr when I made the choice to take things on. Her words fused together into one long, low tone humming in my brain. I didn't believe in psychics but I nearly scratched the skin under my thumb nail off in fear that somehow this woman might know something about Mama.

Maybe it was about the audacity that I decided, even all those years later, what Sadie should be allowed to know about Mama? I had the gall to feel bitter about having no one but the dead to share the truth with when I knew better than anyone that the dead and their secrets still find a way to us.

The truth about Mama filled my mouth and eyes with a stinging saltiness that overshadowed everything good about her. I couldn't remember her easy laughter or her soft palms wrapped around my tiny hands. When Sadie remembered and tried to share it, every muscle in my body tensed up and my forehead ached. The pounding in my ears accelerated until it went silent, like I'd been pulled out of the moment and dunked deep under water.

Evelyn pointed at the last card. Thank God, this was almost over.

I tried to focus on her words. "This card is the outcome you can expect: Ten of Wands. You've been carrying a heavy burden, Mia; I was right. You don't need to carry it all on your own." Her words melted over me like perfect truth. "It's time to rest. You don't have to be the bridge. Love is the bridge." I could feel hot tears running down my cheeks. I closed my eyes to be in the dark with what she said. "Rest. Mia. It's time to lay this burden down and rest."

30. JESS

Watching the tears run down Mom's face, I struggled with the conflicting feelings of relief that Evelyn cracked something open and concern that this whole thing had been a bad idea.

Evelyn's eyes remained closed as she spoke. I didn't think she or Sadie realized that Mom was upset. "There is the presence of a mother energy here that is repeating the same message of the cards. Could this be your mother?"

Mom sat silently, but Sadie spoke quickly. "Yes, it could be. I hope so. What do you see?"

"I see her in a garden. How did your mother die?" Evelyn asked.

Sadie answered, "She had an accident in the garden and died of sepsis. She slipped away before anyone could realize how bad it was."

"She's showing me that she's lying down there, rubbing her arms. She's showing me a bush with pink flowers on it." Mom went pale. Evelyn continued, "There's a man, offering her a blanket."

"Mom, are you okay?" I whispered.

Sadie concentrated on Evelyn's words and didn't notice my mom. "Are you in contact with our mother right now, Evelyn? Is she trying to give you a message for us? The man is probably our father; he died earlier this year. Are they together?"

I kicked my mom gently under the table, but she didn't respond. She slumped in the chair and rubbed the St. Christopher medal around her neck with her thumb and index finger.

Evelyn answered, "She's alone right now. I believe that your mother is showing me something about her time here before she passed."

Sadie continued, "They were devoted to each other."

"No." Mom calmly spoke up, eyes fixed on the table. "They weren't."

Sadie shot Mom a confused look. "What are you talking about Mia?"

Evelyn said, "Mia, I believe your mother is trying to communicate something to you."

Sadie looked from Mom to me. "Daddy did nothing but recount their love story for our whole lives. You read the diary. Jess, help me out here. What impression did you get?"

Evelyn's eyes stayed on Mom. "She's pointing to a window above her. Do you know what she's referring to?"

Mom spoke in such a calm and measured way that it sent a chill up my spine. "You're right about one thing, Sadie. She slipped away before anyone realized how bad things were. After she died, Daddy only remembered what he wanted to remember. Her death allowed him to shape their story in whatever way he chose."

Sadie squinted her eyes and leaned toward her sister. "They did love each other, Mia—written in Mama's own words. Maybe it's not as black and white as I made it out to be but that doesn't make it any less true."

I never saw my mom that upset, not even after Mark died. She seemed eerily calm but something bubbled under the surface. Poor Evelyn sat silently.

Mom spoke slowly and deliberately. "I'm sorry, Sadie." She quieted her voice and looked at Sadie with so much tenderness. "Mama's death wasn't an accident. She got pregnant again and took her own life."

Sadie looked at me, confused, as if Mom spoke a language she didn't understand.

"I heard her and Nana arguing. She felt like a prisoner. That's what Mama said, Sadie. She didn't want another baby. I'm not sure she wanted us." Mom's voice broke at the end of the sentence.

Grandpa must've known that Deenie was pregnant when she died, but no one ever spoke of it. I reached across the table for Mom's hand.

"She wanted to end the pregnancy, but Nana wouldn't hear of it. She wouldn't help her." Mom started sobbing. "And I saw her, Sadie, that's what this woman is talking about; I saw Mama from our bedroom window covered in her own blood, but Mrs. Carini found her and tried to save her." Elbows on the table, she put her face into her hands. "They stopped the bleeding but she found a way to die anyway. Daddy spent our whole lives spinning the tale of this great love story when *he's* the reason she gave up. He left her alone in Presston like he said he'd never do."

I got up and grabbed a box of tissues from the coffee table, putting them in front of Mom.

She blew her nose and turned toward Evelyn with an uneasy expression, like she remembered that Deenie's spirit might still be lingering somewhere in the room. "Maybe the infection traveled into her blood and killed her after a few days but it wasn't an accident." She looked back at Sadie. "Maybe she finished the job later; how would we know? I'm so sorry, Sadie. I'm so sorry."

No one said a word for a full five minutes. Then Sadie calmly got up, pulled an envelope out of her purse, and walked over to hand it to Evelyn. She whispered something in her ear and walked her upstairs.

I glanced up at Evelyn as she left, and tried to smile with my eyes, mouthing, "Thank you."

My mom went to the bathroom and blew her nose. I sat speechless, feeling out of place in the middle of something intimate between the sisters but hoping that my presence might feel like support.

Sadie walked back downstairs, expressionless. Mom came back weeping. I did the math in my brain trying to figure out her age when she saw her mother that way. A nine year-old girl shouldn't have to carry that on her own. For the first time it occurred to me that her fussing over me and my choices may have had very little to do with me.

Mom looked up at her sister. "Sadie, I'm so sorry. I only wanted to protect you. I don't know what happened to me today. Evelyn talked like Mama was here with us and it…"

Sadie interrupted, "Mia. It's going to be okay." She took a deep breath. "This is a lot to process, but all that I can think about right now is the pain in your eyes and I want to help make it better." Mom wept as Sadie wrapped her arms around her.

Sadie said, "I'm sorry that you had to carry this alone."

Mom said, "The sound that came out of Mama that night—the way she struggled to catch her breath, I should have called Nana after she left and made her come back."

Sadie started crying too. Waves of sadness that had been stuck in the darkest places inside pushed out of their bodies as they spoke it into the air around us. Sadie had questions, but she'd wait until later. That was her way.

31. MIA

Earlier today, three crows flew over the house from the back while I prayed for Nana Wanda. Their caws echoed through the trees as they followed one another across the sky and disappeared behind the spire of St. Philip's church. I pulled the red and purple shawl that I knit for myself around my shoulders as a crisp breeze blew through the porch. It felt less like the end of August and more like autumn.

You know how I feel about the fall, Mark. I don't mind the quiet of winter, but I'm usually sad when summer's over and it's time to go back to work. I miss seeing the girls every week and watching the garden come back to life. Autumn is wind and rain pulling it all apart before the inevitable hush of winter. One autumn, long ago, I watched my brilliant Mama, who flourished alongside her red dahlias, lose color, wilt, and fold into herself like her beautiful flowers.

I don't mind telling you that I'm tired of this summer and I welcome its end. Sadie left for a conference in Nova Scotia and decided to do a week-long retreat up there at a Buddhist monastery. I got a postcard today.

> August 25, 2009
> Dear Mia, It's beautiful here on the coast of Cape
> Breton. I'm giving myself time to allow everything

to settle. What a year. I'm practicing Tonglen
Meditation-something my teacher introduced me
to. I am breathing in the dark, dusty cloud of your
pain, allowing it to dissolve in the compassion
of my heart, and blowing back to you the cool,
clear light that will alleviate your suffering.
I love you sister dear. Sadie

I felt especially grateful for Sadie's light when I noticed Jess walking up the steps with the breeze in her long wavy hair and a brightness to her eyes that had been missing. She came over to the porch swing and kissed me hello. I offered her some tea from the cast iron pot sitting next to me. Taking a seat on the chair to my right, she wasted no time asking about me and Sadie.

"We're great, honey. Really. We've missed you at Grandpa's," I said.

All of the muscles in her face relaxed. She intended to give Sadie and me a little time alone together. She popped over with her girls during the week to cut flowers and do her share of the weeding. They made a few bouquets for Mrs. Carini and had several tea parties out back together.

"I enjoyed meandering through the neighborhood with the girls and seeing it through their eyes," she said.

I chuckled. "There isn't much to see."

"That's not true, Mom. We made it a little adventure. We found some beautiful stones by the railroad tracks, met new kids at the park, and fed ducks down by the river." She took a drink of tea. "I'm happy that you aren't carrying so much on your own. I talked to Sadie last night and she said that you two are closer than ever."

That really touched me. I feared the fallout from our visit with Evelyn, but it wasn't as tumultuous as I imagined. Saying those words out loud for the first time made them real. It destabilized me and Sadie brought me back to center. I spent so many years worrying about Sadie that it only recently occurred to me that she might know better than I do—that she might help me. She's not perfect, but she's not Deenie.

So anyway, I set my mug down, put my feet up on the swing, and told Jess that I knew, at least since Daddy died, that I needed to be honest with Sadie. I worried that she'd hate me for keeping the truth from her, or maybe hate me for telling her the truth. Nana Wanda would be terrified for Sadie, with her diagnosis and lack of religion, yet Sadie was naturally forgiving, charitable, and wise beyond anything I could hope to be.

Jess smiled with tender eyes. "Maybe there is more than one path to the same outcome?"

I kept going through my tears. "When she learned the whole truth, she only felt compassion, for me and for Mama, and gratitude that she had options that Deenie wasn't afforded." I wiped my eyes and adjusted my headband, asking Jess to follow me into the living room. I had something to give her.

We slipped off our shoes and walked through the foyer to the living room where I handed her the red leather book with "Diary" stamped in gold on the cover.

"It's Mama's—one that I kept. I wanted to protect Sadie but I realized that this wasn't mine to keep from either of you. Sadie gave it back to me a few days ago."

Jess took the book and thanked me for trusting her. She put her arms around me and held me tight, my heart pounding in between us. I owed it to them both to be honest about where our stories began.

"I've been thinking a lot about our story too: yours and mine." I took her hand and led her over to the couch to sit. "I used to think if I did everything right, I could protect you from the kind of sorrow I've felt in life, but that isn't true, is it?"

"Mom." Jess tilted her head.

"I don't want you to waste any more time trying to be perfect. I'm worried about you. I know you've been struggling."

She shook her head. "No. It's better, Mom. It really is. Jake and I are on a good path."

I could tell by the sound of her voice that my expression betrayed my skepticism. She said that they started therapy and made some changes to their routine. They were trying to bring the best parts of their old life into their new life, but I wasn't sure what she meant.

She put her feet up on the couch and faced me. "There are things that I used to love about Jake that somehow became threatening after we had kids. It's unfair to him." She wrapped her arms around her bent knees. "Watching him jump into a creek feels different when the girls are there to watch him break his neck—when breaking his neck means no one's making money. More often than not, I'd scold him and we'd argue, but before the girls were born, I would've laughed, kicked off my shoes, and waded in with him."

It made sense because Jess was older when I met you, Mark. There were things that I loved about you that would have been more of a problem for me if we had small kids. We remembered you sitting outside by yourself every evening after dinner, sipping that seven o'clock scotch.

"If we had the stress of young children, I'd be worried about him drinking every evening and spending money on expensive scotch. I'd probably be resentful that he got that quiet time to himself every evening when I never took it."

She sat forward. "That's exactly it."

I nodded. "As it was, I felt happy for him."

"His 7 p.m. meditation." Jess giggled. She sat back and grabbed her mug. "I remember wanting that for Jake. I'm not sure when his happiness became unimportant to me. Maybe when my happiness became unimportant to me? Everything is for the girls."

She took a long sip and explained that Jake felt alienated from Jess and what she tried to build with the girls.

"I know that I have work to do. If I can't take care of him anymore, the least that I can do is stop making him feel bad about taking care of himself."

"He still needs care, Jessie. There is room for care for everyone," I offered.

"It doesn't feel like there's room, Mom. Maybe that was your experience, but it hasn't been mine."

Through the window to her left, Jess watched two deer snacking on the rhododendron in the corner of the front yard. "I knew what it felt like to have an unpredictable father, and I chose the same type of man to be a father to my kids."

I remember feeling that about Jessie's father. Even when his choices had nothing to do with me, and I was powerless in the situation, I felt attached to them for better or worse. When Mama seemed too happy or too sad, it meant something about us as a family. My father accepted her for whoever she was on any given day, no matter how it impacted the rest of us. I resented his weakness. Sadie viewed it as unconditional love—even strength.

I put my hand on Jess's knee. "Jake's struggles don't mean anything about who you are as a mother. You aren't *allowing* anything to happen. If you stop believing that, you might be able to view his issues with more compassion and less judgment...for both of you."

I finished my tea and put the mug down, trying a different approach. I told her about the days that you were sick, when I could have been kinder. I took it out on you when I felt frustrated with myself for not taking better care of you. What sense did that make?

Jess smiled sympathetically, "Those were hard days, Mom. Weren't you exhausted? No one could blame you for being grumpy. I would daydream about getting in the car and driving far away from all of us."

Oh Mark, I regret those moments of frustration, as if cooking a different dinner would keep the cancer from causing you pain. Viewing the people I love in terms of: *What does this mean about me? What could I have done better?* It created so much judgment. It's taken me more than half of my life to figure that out.

I *was* exhausted but told her that most of the time, it felt like an honor to help in any way that I could. She and Sadie were so supportive; it gave me permission to make everything about you. It felt indulgent to make you my only priority.

"It was painful to watch him struggle." Jess had never shared that before. "I can't imagine how hard it was for you." A loud car horn across the street startled us both and we laughed. "Hell, I daydream about running away on a tough day and trying on a new life with no obligations," she said.

"But Jess, obligations to others are what makes life worth..." The honking car horn stopped me.

She smiled gratefully, "It has nothing to do with how much I love my daughters. I'm trying to escape the pressure I put on myself. I imagine being a single woman. I'd get home from work and cook what I wanted to eat. If I decided to get dressed up to go have a drink at 8 p.m. on a Tuesday, then I would." She seemed far away for a moment. "The thing that gets me is, if I went to that bar and met Jake, I would want him. I'd want him to be with me and no one else. And that would lead us to precisely where we are right now."

Jess held the green tea mug under her nose, breathing in the steam. She reassured me that they were on the right path. "I want what you had with Mark, Mom."

"And if your happiness becomes more important to you, maybe his will as well?"

"I feel very optimistic." She stopped for a second. "It's strange though, I can't shake the sense that he's keeping something from me. It's so subtle, just something in his face when we talk about certain things. I looked at his phone the other day when he was in the shower."

"Jessie."

"It was a strange thing for me to do. And there was nothing. I just felt guilty and silly."

I pointed to the red diary and suggested she take it out back to her favorite tree while I made some more tea.

32. JESS

Walking through the back door at Mom's place, I realized that it had been ages since I'd been alone in that back yard. When I lived there, I spent so many hours lying on the grass, staring at the stars or reading with my back up against one of the big trees. I walked along the edge of the yard and wondered why my mom never planted anything in the great expanse of grass. I wandered over to my favorite black locust tree, whose bark reminded me of an old woman's veiny hands. Its green leaflets were just beginning to break into tiny speckles of yellow. A month later, when these trees dropped their leaves, the limbs would reach up into the sky like an old woman's crooked fingers. A grandmother tree was the perfect place to begin.

Dear Diary,   *August 14, 1962*
For so long, I couldn't escape the shadows. Darkness lingered between every moment of peace, threaded into my joy, and dispersed into the laughter as it left my lips. Lillian and I created some kind of enchantment that banished the shadows. For months, I had so much energy that I couldn't sleep. Then, the bubble burst. The darkness pressed into my chest with such force that it woke me up one morning. Unable to get out of bed, I panicked. There was no room in the shadows for what Lillian and I shared.

I couldn't answer the phone, but flowers from her garden still arrived at the back door. I didn't show up at her house in the evenings, so she came to mine. Paul and Mumma would attempt to beg me, trick me, or shame me into snapping out of it. When that didn't work, they would stay away until it lifted. Lillian walked right through my back door and upstairs to my room where I laid alone. She sat beside me on the floor and reassured me. She would walk beside me on whatever path led to my peace and burn down anything that obstructed our way.

She wasn't afraid of interfering eyes or accusations or consequences. She wasn't afraid of choking on black smoke or running away from the burning heat until she lost her breath. If it had to be done, she wouldn't let me do it alone. She would sit on the floor beside my bed until the shadows lifted, and I humbly accepted that gift.

On the other side of it, I feel a giddy sense of wonder about the universe. Every time I find myself floating along a particularly rough current, something or someone appears just as I am about to go under. I was lost at sea when I met Paul. He pulled me up and opened the door to a whole world outside of me. Just as domestic life swallowed me, I met Lillian. She gave me the garden and opened a whole world within me. Paul and Lillian both saw me, and through them, I remembered myself. DK

Mom brought the tea outside as I finished the first entry.

"Wow," I said, looking up at her as she approached.

"Wow, indeed," she answered back, handing me the full, green mug.

"Do you think that they were in love?"

"I don't know. I don't." She took a sip. "I have a lot of conflicting feelings about this, which is why I kept the diary hidden to begin with."

"How so? The church stuff?"

Mom shook her head. "No, not at all. I remember when she met Lillian. Something felt off with Mama. I don't know. It's a child's memory and a child's jealousy."

I put the book on the grass. "She writes about her like a woman falling in love."

"Mama was always falling in love. Think of Sadie—so romantic. She fell in love with a poem, a film, or a song. She fell in love with the way a flower smelled. She devoured things whole or starved herself. I know she loved your grandpa, in the beginning at least."

"Do you think that Lillian distracted her from an unhappy situation at home?"

She blurted, "That wind is getting chilly and this tea isn't keeping me warm enough."

I stood up and brushed the dirt off of the back of my jeans. "I should be heading back, although I don't know how I'm going to wait until bedtime to keep reading."

Mom kissed me goodbye. "Take the tea with you for the ride home. I'll get the mug next time."

As I drove back home, I imagined what Lillian looked like and wondered if there were any pictures of the two of them together. I imagined what would happen if an intriguing, single, childless woman came into my life, teaching me new things and telling me how beautiful my eyes were. What would I do if I met someone who reminded me that I was an individual worth noticing? I recognized the danger but couldn't help feeling envious.

33. MIA

Now I've done it, Mark. Everything's out in the open—stirring things up, rather than putting anything to rest. I got a postcard from Sadie this morning.

> September 19, 2009
> Dear Mia, Greetings from St. Louis! I spent
> hours online last night trying to figure out what
> happened to Lillian, but without a last name,
> I couldn't find anything. I closed the laptop,
> walked along the riverwalk, and remembered an
> evening that she and Mama took us swimming
> in the river. They said it was too hot to sleep.
> I remember walking back home through the
> woods, dripping wet because they hadn't
> brought towels, and feeling so happy and free.
> Love you, Sadie.

After Mama met Lillian, she stopped hovering somewhere we couldn't reach her. When I touched her, she vibrated with energy. It filled her whole body and spilled out into the room. She became hard to reach in a different way though. I remember the evening Sadie wrote about. We were at Nana Wanda's and Mama arrived late to pick us up because of Lillian.

If I let my eyes unfocus through the steam from my tea mug, I could see Nana at her kitchen table—smoke and steam floating around her mouth and nose. Nana always seemed to be shrouded in smoke. I think she mostly survived on coffee and cigarettes. She came in to sit with us after she caught me in her refrigerator.

"What are you looking for in there, Mia Maria?"

I tried to push in the plastic vegetable drawer as slowly and quietly as possible.

"Are you in the candy drawer?" she asked more sternly.

Nana's vegetable drawers were full of candy bars: Three Musketeers, Milky Way—with any luck, a Chunky bar. I looked up to see her in the doorway.

"Can we have a lady lock?" I asked, pointing to the bread box.

The vegetable drawers only held candy and the bread box held the sweets she bought after church from the bakery. More often than not, she had lady locks. I loved to stick my finger into the crisp, flaky pastry horn—covered in powdered sugar, and scoop out the buttercream.

"You girls can have a sandwich. It's dinner time and your mumma's late. Sit down at the table."

Sadie and I sat quietly while Nana made us each a cheese sandwich. When she opened the fridge to put the mayonnaise away, Mama rushed into the kitchen.

"I'm sorry I'm late. Thanks for feeding the girls." She kissed each of us on the head. "Lillian came over to help me with the garden. I can't believe my good fortune." Mama got the mayonnaise back out of the fridge and started to make herself a sandwich. "She's so smart, Mumma. She knows about plants. She knows about art. She's read poets that I've never even heard of." She wiped her knife clean on the white bread and screwed the mayonnaise lid back on. "Imagine that. I've never had a friend who knew more about poetry than I do." She took a big bite of her sandwich.

Nana said, "You two seem to spend every available moment you have together."

"We do," she answered. "It's wonderful."

"What does Paul think of her?" Nana asked.

"Oh, they get on great. He's happy that I'm happy. He's probably glad to have someone occupy me in the evenings so he can stay out with his buddies and not hear it from me." She took another bite. "She's wonderful company."

"The girls and I went into town on the bus. I expect Sadie will be tired." Nana said.

"Have you ever seen the jewelry Lillian sells in town?"

Nana crossed her arms. "No. But you've told me about it more than once. This Lillian is all you want to talk about anymore. It's strange for a married woman, a mother, to talk about a girlfriend like this. *I* think you'd be better off finding a friend who understands being a wife and mother."

Mama looked injured. I felt sorry for her but wary of Miss Lillian, as Mama introduced her—not that we spent much time with her. She mostly came around when we were with Nana or after we went to bed.

Swimming in the river with them that evening felt like an invitation into Mama's secret world. When I knew that Nana Wanda couldn't see us, I skipped behind Mama into the darkness of the woods. My eyes adjusted as we followed the worn path and the slightly sour breeze off of the river. Further in, housed by shrubs and trees, the air smelled earthy like warm clay and damp moss. Once we reached the railroad tracks, we entered a chamber of cricket song, then the gentle lapping of the water, then Lillian's greeting. Lillian and Mama took off their dresses. Mama turned to us to help us undress and Miss Lillian leaped into the water in her pointy bra and cotton briefs. Mama took each of our hands and walked into the cool water. I'd seen the river angry after a storm—violently tossing whatever it snatched on its path, but that evening, the current flowed gently. When I sat down, it was like slipping under a mirror into the silence.

When we got home from the swim, I heard Mama and Lillian through my bedroom window. Mama's voice trilled like the day of our pancake picnic. Sadie snored quietly in the twin bed beside me, so I tiptoed down the stairs in my nightgown, hoping to be swept up in Mama's joy like that day. When I got to the back door, I could see them sitting on the ground opposite one another. Lillian bent one of her legs and kept the other straight on the ground near Mama, who rested her hand on Lillian's ankle.

Lillian looked up at the stars and said something about disappearing and running off together to somewhere totally different.

Mama lifted her head to the sky and said she imagined things like that. "Somewhere that the air feels different...somewhere with flowers we've never seen or smelled."

Something about Mama's face sent me back to my bed. I never trusted Miss Lillian after that.

AUTUMN

34. JESS

We made apple crisp on the first day of autumn every year. Jake peeled the bright red apples at our white, farmhouse sink and handed them to me, one at a time. Sarah and Amelia squeezed together on a stool at the counter between us, and took turns stirring together brown sugar and oats while I chopped. We were a picture of the family that I always wanted.

Jake handed me an apple and I held onto his hand for a moment until he smiled at me. "I'm proud of us, aren't you? I feel like we're doing so much better." My gratitude spilled out. "The girls look forward to your Sunday morning donut trip all week long."

"Donuts!" Amelia held her wooden spoon in the air.

"Me too." Jake handed a long apple peel to the dog. "Reading with them at bedtime every night puts the day into perspective for me." He turned back to the apples. "Since you started this diary adventure, you've put the parenting books down. You seem more at ease."

"I *feel* more at ease." I handed an apple slice to each of the girls. "I've noticed a difference in you too. You're present, not just here in the background."

He handed me another apple. "I've been trying very hard to leave work at work." He turned his face down toward the sink. "I feel like we've wasted time." A guilty look reappeared and betrayed his forced smile. He changed the subject. "What's the latest with Grandma Deenie?"

The girls oohed and aahed as I added the rest of the ingredients to the big bowl: baking powder, cinnamon, salt, and the butter that had been slowly melting on the stovetop.

"I'm not over the shock of what Mom divulged at the tarot reading. I identified with Deenie in the beginning, but I think that was overly romantic of me." I scraped the contents of the bowl over the cut apples.

Jake helped the girls down and they ran off chasing the dog.

I opened the oven and slid the glass dish inside. "I felt ambivalent about motherhood, but I mostly got in my own way. She struggled to connect with her family and I can't relate to that. It's actually the opposite for me." I turned to the sink to wash my hands. "I feel so intensely connected that it's hard to see myself outside of our family. It feels like I'll cease to exist if I can't keep us on track."

Jake put his arms around me. "But it's not all on you Jess," he said before kissing me.

The girls called from upstairs. I set the timer and we joined them in our bedroom where they waited for us to put on the pilot movie of *Little House on the Prairie* that I'd been promising for weeks. We propped up the pillows and cuddled into the king bed with the dog and our big down comforter. After we watched the Ingalls family cross the high river and established that Jack the dog hadn't drowned, we took a break from the tension to eat our apple crisp in the dining room. Knowing how much I wanted to get back to the red diary, Jake took the girls on a walk to find the first colorful leaves and I settled in with the book.

Dear Diary,   *September 21, 1962*
Lillian and I spent the weekend transplanting Rose of Sharon trees before the cold comes. She seemed unusually quiet and when I inquired, she told me that she was just distracted and thinking about Halloween. She threw a big party for her favorite holiday and went all out with her costume and decorating the house.

"Do you have any candles you can bring? I want to light everything up to give it a mystical feeling—welcome the spirits. Margaret's going to come and read cards. She's the best I know."

"I didn't think that you saw Margaret anymore?"

She complained about her often and when I wanted to get to know her, Lillian insisted I didn't bother.

Irritated, Lillian rolled her eyes. "Margaret is my Halloween friend. We find our way back together this time of year. I know it'll fade by Christmas so I just enjoy it while it lasts."

She made her sound like a holiday pin that she trotted out to the table by the market for a limited time. I wouldn't like to be a holiday pin in someone's life.

I pushed it to the back of my mind and told her some of my ideas for costumes. We finished work and went back to her kitchen to make hot toddies, spending the rest of the afternoon making plans for her party.

We hadn't been spending as much time together, though we talked every day. Over the summer, she and her mother started setting their table up at a couple other spots around the city, but I looked forward to settling into the cold winter together with warm drinks and long talks. DK

Dear Diary,   *December 2, 1962*

The weather changed but things with Lillian haven't. It's strange. I brought over her mom's favorite cookies and Lillian accepted the box through the screen door without inviting me in. The feigned gratitude felt empty.

She stopped asking for my opinions. She no longer asked about my daughters or the book in my purse. When I offered that information, she seemed disinterested, even annoyed. She didn't care to hear about my problems with Paul anymore. "I'm sorry to hear that," she might offer, before changing the subject.

I explained the perceived change in our friendship and she answered condescendingly. "Darling you can't expect our friendship to be what it was at the beginning. That was just a honeymoon phase."

She didn't have the time she once did to sit around listening to music and talking for hours, she explained. I wasn't concerned with the amount of time we spent together, only with how different it felt when we did. The Lillian that I spend time with now isn't a person with whom I would be vulnerable; she's a girl at the bar every Friday night who enjoys the same music or someone from high school that I'd meet for coffee. This Lillian shouldn't know the things about me that she does. DK

The door burst open with the energy of two little girls and the colors of autumn. Spilling leaves from their arms as they ran toward me, Jake followed behind and offered to make me a cup of tea while Sarah showed me her treasures. Amelia rubbed her cheeks with a torn piece of the lamb's ear that grew near our back door.

"How's the diary going?" he yelled from the kitchen.

"I think I've reached the fall of Lillian."

I suggested to Sarah that she and her sister use glue sticks to add the colorful leaves to our mosaic poster board on the table and the girls ran off.

Jake walked in holding a steaming, yellow mug and leaned down to put it on the table beside me. "Clearly, you need to keep reading."

The girls ran back and forth, gathering spilled leaves and bringing them to the table to add to their project. Jake sat in the overstuffed chair near the dining room to keep an eye on their progress and opened a book about the Stoics. I turned the page in the diary to a letter written to Lillian.

Dear Lillian,   *February 6, 1963*
I feel like I've done something to make you more guarded with me. There are new, unspoken rules in place about what you'll discuss. You seem uncomfortable in my home. When I made dinner, I set aside some of the cabbage soup you love, but you declined. A few days ago, in an effort to reach you, I suggested we plan a fun outing together, just the two of us.

Yesterday, over coffee at your house, you explained, "Deenie, I told Mother what you said, about making plans to do something fun together, and I just couldn't pinpoint why it made me uncomfortable. She said maybe it was the pressure or expectation that put me off."

That's how you express what you don't like about something I do or say. You can't just tell me directly; it feels so disingenuous. The more honest I am, the less honest you are; now I find myself reading into everything you say. You started talking about ideas that you planned as if we hadn't discussed doing those very things together. Then you started living out our plans with other friends: a portrait you painted of your neighbor Jane, a trip to New York with Margaret, and a new cocktail we were going to try with Kevin, your artist friend. You told me about all of it, with no acknowledgement that we planned to do those things together.

I realized something about your character: you're a phony. It bothered me that you spoke about your other friends in such a cruel way but continued the relationship. It makes me wonder what you say about me now that our "honeymoon phase" (your words) is over.
Deenie

Dear Diary,   *February 18, 1963*
Tonight, I confronted Lillian. I told her that she gave the impression that this friendship ran its course and I wanted her to know that she didn't have to pretend.

She denied that anything changed. "Deenie dear, this makes me sad to see you upset. I wasn't expecting this." She looked confused when I gave examples. "Oh, that? I didn't think you could get away for that trip." She had a similar answer to every issue I proposed. It would break her heart to lose me. I had to understand that it wasn't personal. Her life became chaotic but it was temporary. We would get things back to where they'd once been.

She smiled at me warmly and put her hand on mine in a familiar way. Maybe I had been too sensitive? Tonight I glimpsed the old Lillian for the first time in a long time. I felt so relieved that I took her at her word. DK

In the next few entries, Deenie didn't mention her family but described time with Lillian on her birthday and planning the next year's gardens. They spent the first day of spring together and in the summer, she mentioned seeing her less because Lillian and her mom were working more. She alluded to things not being quite the same, but seemed to believe that it was temporary or they would at least evolve to something new. I almost reached the end, so I closed the book, finished my cold mug of forgotten tea, and joined my daughters at the table.

35. JESS

On the day we planned to put the garden to bed, Mom went back to Presston early to have some time alone in the house. We found her at the kitchen table, paging through an old copy of *The Joy of Cooking*, with boxes at her feet.

"Planning a special meal?" I asked, leaning down to kiss her cheek.

"I'm trying to find a stuffed cabbage recipe. Remember Nana Wanda's stuffed cabbage, Sadie?"

Sadie scrunched her nose. "It was pretty bland. I think you can do better." Her mouth dropped open. She reached down for the mug beside my mom. "Where did you find this? Isn't it?"

"Mama's? It was in the very back of the cupboard."

A long time passed since Sadie touched anything that belonged to her mother.

"I wish she was still here."

Mom looked conflicted about how to respond. "We haven't laid eyes on that coffee mug since we were kids."

Sadie didn't speak, slowly rubbing her thumb over the red rose pattern on the mug.

The longer Sadie stayed quiet, the faster Mom's finger tapped the table in front of her. "Whenever I miss her, I immediately resent it though. It's astounding to me that one pancake picnic or a sweet conversation on the porch lasts longer than all of the sad stuff." She ran her hand across the dust on the smooth, cool formica. "We can't pretend that she was a saint just because she's dead."

Sadie handed the mug back to Mom, gathering herself. "No one thinks she was a saint but holding on to pain doesn't make my life better." She sat down and started picking through a box on the floor between them.

Ever since she shared the whole truth about Deenie, Mom's been waiting for Sadie to fall apart. Though she tried to be better, she couldn't help but steer Sadie's emotions into neutral territory. I crouched down to look through a box and picked out a crocheted coaster. Sadie lit up. She made it at Nana Wanda's knitting circle.

"Some would think Mama's love wasn't enough, but it's how she loved." Sadie smiled up at Mom, teasing, "Some might see your love as *too* much, but we accept it's how you love."

Mom laughed. We both appreciated Sadie's ability to lighten the mood.

Sadie rubbed my back. "And look at our Jess, she's the best of us all."

Mom smiled down at me. "If I don't do another thing in this life, I put one incredible person into the world who made it a better place. She looked up at Sadie. "That wasn't enough for Mama, and I can't understand why."

Sadie cocked her head to the side. "You don't think she wished it was enough? I think she did."

"All I know is, I don't think my way is the right way anymore," Mom said, shaking her head. "I'm not sure there is a right way."

Sadie stood up, having found nothing else of interest. "The pressure that society puts on mothers from the moment they discover they're pregnant—judging a woman's conduct for the rest of her life as if it belongs to her children from the moment they're conceived. She's supposed to stop making mistakes, stop learning who she is and what makes her happy—stop being human really. That's why I couldn't even attempt it."

Sadie picked up the crocheted coaster. "And think of Nana Wanda, a single mother in the 1930s?"

"We all keep trying to fix the mistakes of the woman before us but there are always new mistakes," Mom said.

Sadie stopped and walked over to me, putting her hands on my shoulders. "We remember more of the good than the bad, because they were more than their mistakes. And I have news for you ladies, so are we."

Mom stood up. "Are we ready to put this garden to bed 'til spring?"

We followed her out back where she'd already laid out the tools. I worked at cutting back the bee balm and lilies while Mom and Sadie pulled out the last of the annuals.

I waited for the right moment to bring up the diary. "Well, clearly, we have to talk about the red leather elephant here."

Sadie raised her eyebrows. "Have you started reading it?"

"I have, and I'd like to hear what you both think of it all." I measured my words. "How are you doing with everything, Sadie?"

"I'm grateful," she said, "for further illumination of Mama. But I wouldn't mind a little more, Mia. What do you remember about Lillian? She seemed even more important than I thought."

Mom fought the urge to escape and continued working as she spoke. It seemed to her that Lillian disappeared as suddenly as she arrived. She assured us that she didn't know anything more than we did from reading the diary; she didn't even know her last name.

She said, "Nana Wanda was suspicious of Lillian. Naturally, I followed her example, but we didn't spend much time with her. When she came around, she seemed kind." She stood up and grabbed the garden rake, dragging a dozen perfectly parallel lines into the soil where the annuals used to be. "I'm sure I felt threatened; she took up so much of Mama's time and attention. I heard Mama say something once about wishing they could run away."

I didn't remind her that I shared a similar sentiment with her the last time we were together.

She tried to explain, "I have a hard time separating *Deenie* from Mama. I don't know how to see her without the coloring of my expectations, especially now that I've been a mother. I have such strong feelings about the choice to be a mother and the obligations that come with that choice."

"But she didn't have a choice, Mia," Sadie said softly.

We worked quietly after that until Sadie stood up, dragged a bucket of compost over from the edge of the garden, and asked Mom to continue.

"So anyway, then something changed. We spent more time at Nana's. Mama wore the same blue dress every day, with the ripped seam at the bottom and threads hanging down. She stopped wearing lipstick. Daddy and Nana both acted like nothing changed, but I knew. I couldn't reach her, no matter how I tried. She stayed in her room all day and in the garden all night."

I took my gloves off. "Did it have something to do with Lillian?"

Sadie looked up from the begonias she pulled. "I don't think so."

I turned around to see Sadie on her knees, wiping away tears with the back of her gloved hand. A pile of tuberous begonias drooped from her other hand, the once blazing red outline of the pale pink petals tinged with depleted browns.

"Lillian met a vulnerable Deenie. I think it made Lillian seem more important than she actually was." She wiped her cheeks again. "I recognized Mama's sadness. I think that somewhere inside, I knew her death wasn't an accident." She turned toward me. "That could have been me, in another time."

A strong wind blew through, clanging Mrs. Carini's windchimes behind us. Sadie dropped the begonias and sat down on the ground. She pulled her gloves off as tears ran down her cheeks.

Mom pulled off her garden gloves, walked over to her sister and pulled her up. "I'm so sorry, Sadie. I'm so sorry." She wrapped her arms around her. "Jessie, get over here."

I got up and wrapped my arms around the two of them.

"Mama's garden used to feel like an obligation—the burden of keeping her legacy alive. Now I see the way it's brought us together and what a gift that's been." Mom hugged tighter.

As the wind whipped around us, I smiled, knowing that we were Deenie's real legacy. Behind us, to the west, dark clouds assembled near the horizon.

36. JESS

The birds that sang me awake all summer long were busy elsewhere on that crisp October morning—huddling together to keep warm or following the sun. I wrapped myself in a blanket and carried a steaming mug of green tea outside with me. Watching the leaves floating down around me like snowflakes, I breathed into the mug with my mouth open, so the warmth of the hot tea rose up and covered my nose. As I neared the end of the diary, I read in short bursts to stretch it out and savor the building tension in its pages.

Dear Diary,   *October 12, 1963*
A few weeks ago, on a warm September evening, Lillian and I sat on the porch glider together, facing one another as we had a hundred times before. She seemed distracted. I didn't want to intrude, so I rested my hand on her crossed ankles, propped up beside me, and respected the silence.

Finally, she spoke. "My mother is very sick. I don't think that I'll be able to come by in the evenings after tonight."

My mind spiraled in different directions. "You can rely on me," I assured her. "I want to support you in any way I can."

Lillian stared off toward the streetlight by the park, and I didn't know what else to say.

"I can come to you. I can bring dinners and groceries—whatever you need." I held on to her ankle, gently floating my thumb back and forth over the skin, wanting to hug her but sensing it wasn't the right time.

She met my eyes briefly. "Thank you, Deenie. You're sweet."

"Sweet" felt like a pat on the head. When I couldn't get out of bed and she sat next to me, I would never have described it as sweet. She walked beside me through murk and shadow.

After that night, it became increasingly difficult to reach Lillian. When I called to check in, she spoke politely but changed the subject when I asked about her mother, who I assumed must have been listening nearby. When I could get away, I went to her place to listen to music together after her mother went to sleep, but she still didn't want to talk. Eventually, she stopped answering the phone.

Then, last night, on a chilly October evening, I drove over after the girls went to bed. She seemed surprised to see me, as if it wasn't something that happened all the time. Through the screen door, she inquired about my children and my health. I couldn't sit beside her, offering the quiet support she once offered me, because she wouldn't even open the door.

She looked into my eyes as if staring through a window. I decided to aim directly for her heart. My previous attempts at quiet support and encouragement fizzled between us.

"I miss you, Lilly. I'm worried about you. I want to be here for you." The sound of her telephone ringing from the kitchen distracted me. "I miss hearing about your day—the painting you're working on or the book you're reading." It seemed odd that anyone would call at that hour. After three rings, it stopped. "I just want you to know that I feel the absence deeply, because you're important. I miss knowing what's weighing on your heart. I want to be here for you."

"I miss you too, but I'm overwhelmed, Deenie. I'm doing the best that I can."

"Can I help?" The phone started ringing again.

"You're sweet. I'm sorry. I have to go." The screen door squealed as she leaned out through the small opening to kiss my cheek and *closed before I could say anything more. I pulled my thick cardigan sweater together around my neck and walked back toward the car in a fog.* DK

I closed the book and held it against my chest. *Sweet* was my white-haired neighbor with the toothy smile who baked cookies whenever a new neighbor moved in. I called my child *sweet* after she shared her ice cream with her sister. When a person is forced to walk through hell, there are people who will walk beside them and people who won't. That's nothing like cookies and ice cream.

It made sense that Mom kept the diary from us. It would be easy for the reader to think that no one but Lillian mattered to Deenie. Sadie wouldn't read it as the rejection that Mom did; she only wanted to know her mother as a full human being in all of her triumphs and struggles. We don't all get to know our mothers that way. I thought I did, but I didn't.

More than anything, my heart hurt for Deenie—confused and alone in her grief with no one to witness what she had and lost with Lillian. Nana Wanda would still take the girls and might tell Deenie to stop being dramatic. Grandpa would stay out late at night and imagine he was at fault for Deenie's melancholy.

I couldn't understand her loss, but I understood feeling lonely in your life, even with two beautiful daughters and people who love you.

37. DEENIE

L et me tell you a story from the cold wind flying through the treetops, tempting the colorful leaves to surrender with prom- ises of a journey somewhere new. Lillian grew flowers in every shade of red. For three summers, I came home to her bouquets on the back doorstep. Carefully chosen and arranged from whatever bloomed in her yard, she punctuated the display with a statement flower: an allium with its explosion of purple petals, or a hibiscus flower the size of my hand—white with red interior bleeding out into the border of the petals and a fuzzy yellow pom pom shoot- ing forth from the center.

For two autumns and two winters, we took blankets and warm drinks to the front porch and read tarot cards. We walked by the river on snowy evenings and made plans. In the spring- time, we dug up lilies of the valley—broad green leaves hiding delicate white paper bells, and blue green hostas that peeked out from the ground of her front yard like the tip of a rocket launching from within the soil. We planted them all in a sun-dappled spot behind my house. I wove the rhythm of my days into Lillian's. When she started pulling away the autumn that her mother got sick, I lost my footing.

She had parties, around the holidays, during brief peri- ods when her mother felt better. Paul and I would chat with the ever-changing parade of strangers that she seemed to attract but I could never get Lillian alone for more than a five-minute conversation. She surrounded herself with strangers, old friends who wouldn't ask questions, and anyone who might distract her from her pain, but she wouldn't speak to me.

She floated around her party, laughing and singing, but her eyes were glossed over and puffy. Whenever I approached her, all of my offers of support, along with so many unexpressed words and feelings, tipped back and forth between us—precarious and cumbersome, and threatened to flatten the person standing on the wrong side.

Before we left her party, I grabbed her hands. "Everything must feel like a lot right now. Maybe the best way for me to help is just to give you a little more space?"

"Should I ignore all of my guests and just pay attention to you?" she asked.

I didn't say "of course not" or explain the difference between what I asked and what she answered. I just excused myself.

"You aren't going to pout now, are you?" She put her hand on my elbow and forced a smile. "Just because I don't spend the whole party talking to you doesn't mean that you aren't the most important person here."

I kissed her on the cheek and went home.

If I showed up, she felt smothered; if I pulled back, she felt rejected. So I stood still. I busied my hands when they tried to pick up the phone and stopped my legs from carrying me to her door when I imagined her suffering alone, though I couldn't be sure that she was alone. I didn't know anything because she wouldn't tell me anything.

I stopped going to the parties because being close enough to smell her but seemingly invisible constricted my throat until my lungs burned. Then I stopped calling, because chatting about the weather was playing a part. Once I stopped calling, there was nothing left. I read Neruda's Sonnet LXV and waited to be seen again. I questioned my own sanity more than I usually did, certain that I mistook every moment of our relationship and perceived something that never existed. Mumma's words took hold of me. It wasn't normal for a married woman with children to feel the way I felt about Lillian.

So, I waited.

I waited for a different scent from the thick, ancient wisteria vines in the woods. I waited for the red roses in my front yard to bloom yellow. I tasted every apple that next autumn expecting something different from the clean, crisp fruit filling my mouth. If my perception could be trusted, why hadn't she felt the void?

After her mother's death, she told me at the funeral that she moved to an apartment in Uptown beside the fire station. I saw her once, animated and laughing, leaving the movie theater with a group of friends I'd never seen before. She pretended not to see me. I wondered if she was angry with me for abandoning her. Had I abandoned her? I couldn't remember. I couldn't keep it straight. The more time that passed, the less sure I felt about anything that happened between us.

38. MIA

I know this won't come as much of a surprise, but I'm worried about Sadie. Ever since I admitted the truth about Mama, I've been waiting for her to…oh, I don't know, have a response? Sadie seemed to be treading water but this postcard I got today seemed strange.

> October 16, 2009
> Dear Mia, I made it to Flagstaff. You wonder
> why Jessie wants to know about Mama? Why
> do humans honor their ancestors? We hope
> they guide us from beyond. We want to feel
> a sense of belonging or a connection to the
> past. We want to understand the thread that
> weaves through time. How can Jess know
> you without knowing Mama? How can you
> and I really know ourselves? Love, Sadie

I decided to call her. I typically tried not to bother her when she traveled but the tone of that postcard made me anxious. She greeted my call with laughter, saying she figured she'd hear from me and I wasn't entirely out of line. So far, she kept the distorted thoughts under control.

"This is when I utilize the tools I've learned, Mia," she told me. "You have to give me a little space to try."

She assured me that she took her meds and talked to her therapist. She would be on a plane home the next day and she'd come see me first thing.

"You know what's odd?" she said. "You aren't the only call from home I've received on this trip. Jake called me. He left a message to call him back, but when I tried, he didn't answer. Maybe he has something planned for Jess?"

"Maybe?" I answered. "Let me know what you find out."

39. JESS

I buttoned my sweater as I walked out of the grocery store that day, holding canvas bags full of everything we needed to start a season of soups and hot chocolate, movies in bed, and reading by the fireplace. Feeling more confident in my little life, I made plans for a better winter together with Jake and the girls.

Sarah usually heard my keys in the door and came to inspect the grocery bags for treats, but no one greeted me in the kitchen. I walked into the warmly lit dining room to find Jake waiting with dinner for two, eyes wide and breathing shallow.

"Sadie took the girls to your mom's for a sleepover," he said as I sat down.

I could tell from his energy that it wasn't a romantic surprise.

"You're just in time," he said. "I made you dinner for a change. Tell me what you think."

I cut the stringy, limp, asparagus into small bites. "What's going on?"

"Jessie, I've gone back and forth about telling you this, but we've worked so hard. It feels important to move into the next part of our lives with complete honesty. I realize this might ruin everything, but I want you to understand how committed I am to you and our family. I'm so sorry." His voice shook. "It sits in the corner of every wonderful moment we have and corrupts everything I'm trying to do to be better for you and the girls and I am so, so sorry." Tears trickled down both of his cheeks. "I'm praying that you will still choose me, in spite of who I can be and what I've done, but if you can't, then I don't deserve you."

It was purely circumstantial—the betrayal of our vows. Last winter, when things were bad, he found himself alone with *Tracy from Sales*. Beat down from another fight with me that morning and lifted up by the fourth drink, I imagined that he escaped the tension waiting at home through curtains of blond hair, deep red nails, and skin that smelled like a tropical vacation.

He felt sick. It only happened once and would never happen again. He wanted to be honest because we worked so hard to fix things. He didn't want any secrets. His words slid into one another and rearranged themselves in my brain. In the middle of a bite, I forgot how to swallow. My throat closed around the food. There was no room for food, or breath, or words to speak back to his revelation. As he went on and on, something dark seeped in, like water under a door, accumulating into a force that threatened to pull me under.

"You have to go right now, or I have to go." I stood up and spit the chewed asparagus into a napkin.

He looked confused and begged me to sit down and talk.

"I'm leaving. I can't talk about this anymore tonight."

"Where are you going?" he called as I left the room.

From the kitchen, I told him not to wait up and grabbed my sweater.

"Jess."

"Jake!" I interrupted. "Will you please give me a fucking minute? Your words don't make any sense to me right now. Nothing makes sense."

I ran outside, forcing air into my lungs and moved up the hill at the end of our street without a plan, taking slow deep breaths through my nose. The smell of pine trees and the steely edge of the wind were a welcome reprieve from Jake's overcooked vegetables, wet eyes, and suffocating shame. I squeezed and unsqueezed my hands like a heartbeat. It wasn't the time to go numb and detach. I walked toward a better view of the crescent moon and tried to wrap my brain around his words.

I used to assume that great wisdom accompanied age and looked forward to getting older, but I didn't consider that older people were also more beaten down by life. I accounted for a slim chance of interruption by fate but I didn't account for the million tiny heartbreaks that happen: the pain of marriage and relationships, of disappointment in self and others, or the fact that even when you do everything right, it can still go wrong.

My mind settled on what seemed like the deeply flawed men in my life. My grandfather Paul, so warm and generous to me, put his young family at risk to fill some empty space and allowed his own pain to blind him to the pain of the ones he loved the most. My father, more invested in escaping his shame than anything else, and my husband, spiraling through stress and desperation—all of them drinking too much. I thought about the women responsible for keeping it all together when the men bailed. How could I judge anyone when I dreamed of escape?

I started running. When I couldn't run any longer, I walked into the darkness of a little park nearby and laid on a patch of grass. I studied the limb of the tree directly above me with its leaves in various states of autumn glory: one green leaf just beginning to turn, a few of them the lightest red, and a few blazing. Behind me, crabapples littered the ground filling my nose with the rotting sweetness of earthly decay.

The earth didn't care when my life imploded and it blanketed me with peace. The leaves would turn and fall and everything would go brown and quiet, no matter what happened. The crescent moon was timeless, just like Deenie's strawberry moon. The earth was timeless and I was just a visitor. The weight of guilt and expectation lifted a little, feeling the insignificance of my choices. I stayed there for a long time, breathing easier, until the wind blew in a chill that stung the tip of my nose.

I walked the rest of the way back, thinking of all the ways that Jake had been trying to make things better the last few months. One morning when he snapped at me as he grabbed his bag to leave for work, he dropped the bag, went upstairs, and changed his clothes. He came downstairs and asked if we could start the day over. After a stressful day at work, he asked for time alone to take a bath and reset before he spent time with us. He sat down to dinner that night, present and happy. He made time with the girls. We made time for each other.

As I turned onto our sidewalk, I noticed the entire first floor of our home lit like a beacon from down the street. Inside, I cautiously looked around for any sign of Jake. The bedroom door upstairs was closed, so I assumed that he'd gone to bed. My mind felt hazy, clinging to the idea that everything that happened before I left had been a dream.

I took a bottle of wine outside and made a fire in the fire pit. Two glasses in, I tried to remember her face. I'd only met *Tracy from Sales* once, briefly, at a Christmas party. Compelled to visualize the two of them together, I grabbed my laptop to look her up. I studied her cheeks, her ears, and her hands. I imagined his hands in her hair as he kissed her. Where did it happen? The next time I took off my clothes, did he compare my body to hers?

There were times last winter that I wanted out of our marriage but I never anticipated the terror that accompanied the opportunity at my door. I didn't want him to be someone else's partner. We were a family. I finished the bottle and noticed the clock: midnight. I went upstairs.

I listened through the closed door. The door stuck as I turned the knob, but the bark as it opened didn't disturb the pattern of his snoring. Seeing my husband in our bed, I felt surprised by my softness. I kicked off my shoes and took off my shirt, wanting to feel his skin on mine. He opened his eyes with a look of both trepidation and relief. The jumbled words and emotions that had been bouncing off the inside of my skull cleared. Moved by something pulling deep within my chest, I climbed on top of him and sunk the weight of my body into his.

I whispered into his ear, "I'm going to ask you some questions and I want you to answer them and trust me."

I could sense his anxiety but also the peace of this familiar comfort as we clung to each other.

"Was there a moment when you looked at her or touched her and realized what might happen if you kept going?" I asked.

He didn't answer.

"I need you to be honest and trust me." I needed to know everything, to know if I could live with it.

"Yes," he whispered.

"Where were you?" Kissing his neck softly after I asked, I felt something like desire as a coping mechanism. I didn't know if I meant to reclaim my territory or torture myself, but I needed to feel something besides the excruciating sensation of my ribcage being slowly pulled apart from the center. I needed to be as close as possible to him while I heard these details.

"In her living room." Half-asleep, he put one hand on my back and used the other hand to stroke my hair.

"How did you end up in her living room?" I kissed his ear lobe and breathed him in.

"She left paperwork there that I needed for the weekend." He seemed confused but also grateful to be close. I put my hands on his face and started to kiss him so that the harder we kissed the more lost I might become in his body. He put both arms around me and pulled me in as close as he could.

His regret pulsed against my chest. The intrusive thoughts that fled when I entered the room rushed back in. I put my forehead on his shoulder and started sobbing.

"Why didn't you leave? Why did you even go there? The moment you knew it could happen—why didn't you stop?" The words streamed out like one long sentence.

"I'm so sorry. I'm so sorry. I don't know why I didn't leave. I drank too much and got caught up in something that didn't feel real. It felt theatrical—detached from reality. I can't explain it. I should never have gone there. I'm so sorry Jessie. I'm so sorry. I don't want anyone else. I only want you."

I kept my face against the skin of his chest. I needed to feel him without seeing his guilty face or revealing mine. There were things happening between us that contributed to his decision to go into her apartment that night, but I felt grateful that he didn't say it. We managed to let each other down in so many different ways, but he crossed a line that destroyed something sacred between us—something only we shared. Now we shared something different—something ugly and unwieldy. We held onto each other and grieved until the wine, tears, and exhaustion carried me into sleep.

The next morning, I woke up with my back to him and his arms around me, surprised that with a clearer head in the light of day, my instinct was still to be close to him.

"I think you have to go," I said.

"Okay."

At our worst, that previous winter, he wouldn't agree to a trial separation. With his arms around me, I stared out of the bedroom window at the barren tree swaying in the wind.

"I love you so much Jess."

"I know. I love you too."

40. MIA

Dread is a needy companion. It pinched and pulled at me before I wiped the sleep from my eyes this morning and fixed them on the ceiling light above our bed. The hideous frosted glass flower shined from the ceiling the first time we walked into this room and I couldn't understand why you liked it. Why hadn't I replaced it yet?

Sadie showed up at dinnertime yesterday with Sarah and Amelia, under the guise of a surprise sleepover. Jake asked her to take the girls so he and Jessie could talk alone. I know Sadie knows more than she's saying. Jess shares things with Sadie that she'd never tell me. *Overbearing Mia* is their shared joke, instead of giving me any credit for my life experience. I created this one-dimensional character for myself who functioned as their support and not as a woman worth knowing. If Mama hadn't left the diaries, I wouldn't have known her at all.

Looking at myself in the mirror by the bathroom sink this morning, I studied the lines in my forehead and the puffiness under my eyes. Deenie and Wanda both looked back at me. They were in my bones. When I went downstairs to make breakfast, Sadie asked me if I was okay and offered to take the girls back home, but I wanted to give them a little more time.

"Maybe you should pop over and check in with Jess and I'll follow with the girls in a little while?" Sadie suggested.

I agreed. Something didn't feel right, but I couldn't trust my instincts; the impact of the last few months made me question everything. Watching my sister laughing with my granddaughters, the three of them jingling Sadie's jewelry, I felt disappointed in myself for getting caught in the past and missing the present.

After I got ready, I slipped out to the car while Sadie helped the girls get dressed. When I pulled into Jess's driveway and saw Jake's car, I took it as a good sign. After a few deep breaths, I walked up to the door. Jessie opened it with red, puffy eyes and stepped outside to tell me that Jake was leaving for a while. I stood, mouth open, as she told me the details. She seemed so optimistic the last time we talked at my house.

Jessie fell into my open arms and cried from a bleak place within. I held onto her and reassured her that she wasn't alone, feeling my own heart echoing throughout my body. She just hung up with Sadie, who offered to keep the girls so she could try to sleep. She told me to head back home; she would call me later.

I turned and walked back to my car. I couldn't fix this for her; I couldn't even remember the meditation that Sadie wrote about so I could breathe in her suffering or something. As soon as the car door slammed shut, I released the handle and exhaled into deep sobs that reached down low—pulling on my gut and threatening to make me sick. I hadn't protected anyone. I lost so much with Sadie—time to just be sisters and share Mama with someone who understood. I stole that from my sister. I lived my entire adult life for Jessie—to create a better life than I knew, and she still suffered so much.

I drove to Presston. I didn't want to weed Mama's garden and revisit that sadness every year. I didn't want to go through Daddy's things and learn any more secrets. I wanted to be rid of them. I wanted to be rid of it all.

41. JESS

After Jake left, I showered and wrapped myself in layers to shore up the hollow space: a soft, cotton shirt and sweatpants, my favorite brown sweater, and the thickest socks I could find. I made a cup of peppermint tea and took it to the couch, pulled a quilt over my legs, and escaped within the red diary.

Dear Diary,   *September 18, 1964*
It's been a month since Lillian came back to me with bulbs for the garden. I dreamed of her the night before: she sat down beside me, slipped her arm around my waist, and leaned her head toward my neck. I'd forgotten the comfort of trusting her the way I once did—believing her. It stayed with me after I woke up and throughout the morning like I dreamed a salve onto my wounded heart—a wound that had mostly healed but hurt with any kind of pressure.

When she arrived at my house with tired eyes and sunken cheeks, I hoped to feel that same connection. The bones in her back felt sharper when we hugged hello. She fidgeted, telling me a story about the lilies.

When her mother died, she lost her lifelong companion. Every choice she made after that, was a choice to end the life she lived before in order to survive the grief. Even if she chose them, there were more losses: her home, her garden, and me.

Overwhelmed with compassion, I blurted, "I'm sorry for anything I might've done to add to your suffering when you were going through so much. I didn't know how to support you the way you needed me, but I never wanted to add to your distress."

She looked through me, like the night she wouldn't open her door. "I know you didn't want to hurt me. I didn't want to hurt you either." She walked over to the beginning of the garden path that led toward the woods. "This would be a nice spot for the lilies."

She talked endlessly without saying much and left me in a cloud of hollow words. I don't believe either of us found familiar solace that day. Our hearts were left unattended for too long. Everything unsaid lingered between us until it dispersed and scattered into the cosmos.

Even so, I planted the lily bulbs she brought and willed them to grow roots deep into the soil and bind us back together. I prayed a Dickinson poem over the freshly-turned soil: "Show me Eternity, and I will show you Memory." The prayer didn't work.

Last week, I went shopping downtown on a cold afternoon. As the sun set, I walked over to the neighborhood where she lived and found the fire station. I approached the building next door and watched her light come on. Maybe she was welcoming a new friend, or sitting down for a meal, or looking for a book on her shelf. I wondered what she read or if she still painted. Just then she glanced up, but she didn't see me. I closed my eyes, sent her love, and I left.

That's what changed. Is there anything that compares to the pain of being truly seen by someone and then becoming invisible, with no acknowledgement of the moment it happened? One day you are someone and the next, you're no one. It's humiliating.

If I would've been satisfied with small talk at her parties, then I'd probably know what book she was reading. If, like Lillian, I could've watched something sacred unravel and pretend it wasn't happening—or worse, pretend it was never sacred, then we could be the kind of friends who met for coffee every six months to catch up. As it is, we're strangers. She spent the last year carving out a new life for herself and I hadn't been permitted to witness it. I didn't know her anymore; maybe I never did.

And yet, when I walk through my house, I still see her. Every room has something of her in it.

I'm not sure if it's Lillian that I miss now, or if it's being seen. I miss the feeling of myself as someone more. Now I disappear into the walls, into my bed, into the garden, and find what I can. DK

There were a few short entries with no mention of Lillian: lines from poems, run-on sentences that didn't make sense, and brief moments of clarity. Then I came across this.

Dear Diary,   *Sept 29, 1964*
The garden is all I have now. I'm in my body in the garden. I'm connected to something. I'm bound to something. Earlier in the summer, I cut the first roses that bloomed and put them in the ceramic vase that Lillian made for me near the kitchen window. As the roses turned brown, wilted, and shriveled on the windowsill, I tried to remember what it felt like when we met and told myself stories about who she must have been to make sense of the loss.

One morning, I forgot about the roses. I thought of her less and less every day. Last night, I decided to throw them out. When I turned the vase over to dump it into the sink, I read: "To My Beloved" carved into the bottom, in her hand. I couldn't remember if I ever saw that before. I couldn't remember being her beloved. I stood at the sink bellowing, when Paul came through the front door.

Even though I had nothing to offer him, he pitied my sadness. I couldn't remember being his beloved either, but he kept trying. He came home from the bar earlier when the weather started changing and the darkness closed in. Without words, he caught my eyes and knew. He walked over to me and I collapsed into him. The empty spaces ached fiercely inside of me.

I woke up this morning after our first night together in a very long time and remembered, as I did every morning, that I lived the very life I swore I never would. He wanted to give me the life he promised, but we were stuck now. DK

Dear Diary,   *Oct 19, 1964*
I'm convinced that life means to toy with us. It drags us down like ocean waves—scraping us on rough sand and rock and steals the breath from our chest until we panic. At the last moment,

it releases its grip long enough for us to push toward the light and inhale, before we're sucked back down, unless you get lucky and find a life raft.

I thought Lillian was a life raft, but she wasn't. It felt sudden in the beginning but I see now that she deserted me long before her mother got sick. She told me I was being silly when I sensed the shift; I don't know if she was a coward or a fraud. Once her words went hollow, she put me into a box like her old trinkets, waiting to be taken to the table in town to sell to passersby.

The sorrow that held me turned into regret. I felt no gratitude for the love we shared. It dried up like the roses until it disappeared completely, and my heart condensed into something concentrated and impenetrable to fill the empty space. Knowing her didn't make me better; it subtracted something from me. I was less than I was when she met me.

On the third morning that I woke up to vomit, I remembered Paul's enchanted eyes on the night that I threw the roses away. I ached with grief and didn't care that it was the wrong time of the month. This morning, I sat on the bathroom floor and tried to accept what it meant. Another baby and another shackle to this life in this goddamn town. I'll never be free. DK

42. MIA

When I got to the industrial road, I pressed the gas pedal to the floor. On my left, I watched a wasteland fly by—nothing green, only muted shades of gray. The familiar pit in my stomach grew as I got closer to Presston and in my frustration, I gripped the steering wheel tighter.

I could hear her voice, arguing with Nana on that awful night.

"Mumma, I'm pregnant again," she said.

"Oh my." Nana pulled out a chair and sat down.

"I can't have another baby, Mumma. You know how Paul is. We can barely get by as we are. I can't have another baby."

"Well, you don't have a choice, Geraldine. What are you talking about?"

I was supposed to be asleep. In my yellow nightgown, I crouched down on the top step, listening to them argue in the kitchen, while Sadie slept in our bedroom.

Mama said, "I'm talking about Mrs. B. I need you to keep the girls at your house tomorrow night."

"Geraldine, No. It's a sin. No, you can't do that."

"Mumma, I can't have this baby. I won't survive this. Everything's a mess—more than you even know."

"Geraldine, what do you think? I wanted to have a baby alone and go through Presston with everyone's eyes on me?

Do you think that I could have a baby with no husband and no help? But I did. God gave you to me for a reason. A baby is a gift from God."

"You can't be serious?" Mama seemed hysterical at that point. "God didn't give me this baby. I'm useless to the ones I already have. Don't you ever think about what your life might have been if you didn't have me?"

"No, I don't. Because it wasn't an option and it's *not* an option for you. You will *not* go see her, Geraldine. She's old and she doesn't know what she's doing. You're going to get hurt and then who'll take care of your daughters?" Mama growled with a terrifying desperation. Unphased, Nana continued, "If you do this, I cannot look at you. I cannot look after the girls and know that you've chosen this. I will not. You can have this baby, Geraldine. I'll help you." Her voice got softer. "You've been given this baby for a reason."

I turned onto Ohio Street and noticed the cigarette butts littering the ground outside of the bar. An angry dog barked from the front yard across the street. I passed the second bar and the drunk old man who sat on the porch, when I heard the clanging of a broken swing at the park, hitting the metal pole beside it. I pulled in front of the house and followed my anger straight through the walkway, to the back yard, to the shed and Mama's tools.

I grabbed a hoe and a shovel and threw them both down on the ground. I didn't want the garden to be her legacy. If I destroyed it, then it would look like the chaos she really left behind. I fell hard on my knees, ripping and pulling at every green thing around me. I picked up the hand hoe and brought it down with all of my strength, cutting deeply into the soil. I wanted to wound this ground and kill something that she brought to life. I brought the hoe down into the soil over and over again, dragging it toward me, ripping roots apart. Behind me, I noticed Mrs. Carini's kitchen curtain pulled to the side. She saw my mother—crazy in the dirt. I doubled down to exorcize the ugliness.

I moved off of my knees and sat down, dragging dirt across my face as I attempted to wipe the sweat off of my forehead.

More than any other childhood memory, that night replayed vividly in my mind. I looked at the yellowing leaves and shriveled buds around me and realized that it was the same time of year. She put the garden to bed and laid down to die in it.

215

43. DEENIE

Let me tell you a story from a place far beyond the boundaries of human experience, where I am unburdened by the distortions that controlled me in life. It's the way they looked at me. Mumma, rosary jingling in her pocket, didn't recognize me as I pleaded for her help. Paul called me unpredictable, but he didn't say it the way he did when we first met. He sent the girls to my mother while I hovered outside of my body: untouched, unseen, tired...so tired.

They tiptoed around, waiting for me to explode into a thousand floating embers around them. The fear on their faces disturbed me. Who was I to them anymore? Not honeysuckle on their lips, but bitter greens that they chewed and chewed and swallowed so they wouldn't starve.

I got out of bed and wrote a letter to Mia at my vanity. Rifling through the drawers, I found my diaries and the acorn bracelet that Lillian gave me on the day that I learned her name. I ripped the last pages out of my red diary and grabbed the metal bank box from the bottom of the drawer, dumping the coins back inside. I threw my things into the empty box and went downstairs.

When I walked through the backdoor in my nightgown, I'd already decided. I sat down on the ground of my beautiful, exhausted garden between green tomatoes, hopefully curling forward, and sage in the corner, half-yellowed and ready for a long winter's sleep. In the earth, these wearied leaves would feed what came next. Destruction for creation—it made sense.

When I was ten, my mother told me that my babcia died to make room in the world for new babies to be born. Horrified, I imagined whose grandmother died to make room for me. I remembered Babcia Teresa with her frizzy gray hair, pinkish-brown skin tags covering her neck, and booming, angry voice. She fought every day of her life: with her family, her neighbors, and anyone else who crossed her. The day that she died, that terrifying woman smiled with relief. I felt mystified that she wasn't afraid, but later, I understood. She was finally free. There would be no more fighting—only surrender.

Paul said we were visitors, but I think we belong to the earth. In that hellscape of smoke and fiery flare towers, soot-stained faces and hands and homes, I found a plot of land to love. I nursed the tired soil back to life and that night, the earth welcomed me home. I laid on my back, feeling the pull like arms extending from below: not to suffocate, but to embrace. Yielding, I pressed my ear to the warm ground and listened to the deep thrumming of a distant heartbeat. Human bodies went cold, but the earth was alive.

It drew tears from my eyes, salty into the ground, and the thrumming sped up in response. How could I feed this one beautiful thing that I managed to create? With my tears or the drops of milk that leaked from my breast when I imagined another child needing me? I opened the buttons of my nightgown as it beckoned me closer.

Curves and tendrils just beneath the first layer of soil unfurled and tickled my ankles with a caress. Blood red roses slowly danced forward and around the exposed side of my face, licked the tip of my earlobe, seductively swayed beneath my nose. I closed my eyes, dizzy from the scent.

Velvety rose tiptoed across my forehead. The supple ground engulfed me in gratitude and I slipped out of my nightgown. The wind picked up, electric. It moved around me and sprinkled tiny droplets of cold rain like a baptism into my new life. I rubbed it into my skin with the earth.

Exquisite pangs of pleasure resonated in every part of my body. A voice within echoed that I must get closer. I grabbed the shears to my right and slid the point along the tender flesh of my exposed wrists. Pushing my hands into the soil, I felt waves of resounding love as it received my blood. I rubbed the soil into my wrists and along my arm, red paste into every pore. I made a choice to give myself freely.

In my body, the echo, "I am free. I am free." There was no Deenie. There was only dissolution into earth that would feed and nurture the ones who looked to me. There was only that one small place of beauty and nurturing and not taking, taking from tired eyes, calloused hands, and whiskey breath. I changed one small part of that place. That was enough.

Far away—the sound of a woman's voice screaming for Paul, pressure on my wrists, a rough blanket on my naked body, and then I saw her in the window above me: Mia, in her little yellow nightgown.

44. JESS

I glanced up at the clock. Sadie and the girls would be home soon and I couldn't stop reading, knowing that Deenie just found out about the pregnancy.

Dear Diary,   *Oct 23, 1964*
What did I expect from Mumma? She didn't recognize me. She was ashamed of me for wanting to end the pregnancy. After she left, I cried until I was empty. I don't know how to mother these girls without her help. I would be as useless to this new child as I am to my husband and daughters—as I've always been to my mother. I did the best I could. I had the girls and I did my best.

My time with Paul feels like a different life—a different me. I don't know how to get it back after I let go. He meant the promises he made but shackled me here and left me alone. I feel Presston rising up through the black smokey stacks and stalking me wherever I go. I let go of Lillian. She made promises too, implied in a way that she could escape and claim no guilt. She was an illusion and our friendship...a fraud. I let go of my daughters because it's better for them. Motherhood was inevitable but it's not my purpose.

In books, the only thing that matters is the love between people. I want to connect to other people, but it never lasts. Is there meaning to my life if it isn't connected to someone else's? Am I missing something that every other human has?

For as long as I can remember, I've felt happiest in solitude. When I am under the umbrella of the woods or in my garden, I'm bringing something into this world. That's my purpose here: to midwife something I can't see and don't entirely understand. In Utah and in Tucson, when I felt most alive, I was a conduit for something bigger. Maybe it's enough to be a conduit; not everyone is built to see things through to the end. I'm a spark. I ignite.

But when these great loves of mine stand before me, willing me to love them back after I've let them go, the pain is more than I can tolerate. When I search my brain for some escape, I think about the night in the woods, when I couldn't breathe until I disappeared into the darkness. I clutched the thorny bush and bled into the earth. The atoms of my being floated up and into the moonlight and finally there was some peace. I need to find some peace. DK

I closed the red book as Sadie arrived with the girls, floating as one into the house with energy and sweetness. Kisses all around and I got up to run to the bathroom. I waited too long, trying to fit in as much of the diary as I could before their return. Sadie took one look at me holding the red book and cued up a movie for the girls. We met on the back porch once they were settled so I could explain everything about Jake.

"And that's it? He just left?" Sadie asked, reclining on the chaise out back.

"He told the girls he had a work trip," I whispered, hearing their chatter inside the house.

That morning, I listened to him saying goodbye to the girls over the phone—his voice breaking between the words "work trip" and "I'll see you soon." I turned through the hallway with no intention of watching him leave and walked upstairs to disappear into the black abyss of my future.

"What are you feeling?" She put her hand onto mine and I felt grateful for her touch.

"I don't know. I'm surprised that I'm not angry. I'm surprised that I'm not feeling more righteous. I'm surprised about a lot of things." I took a drink of my tea.

I should've protected our marriage. I protected our family for the kids, but when I woke up that morning, I wasn't thinking about them. The grief that clawed from under my skin came from knowing that Jake contaminated something sacred between the two of us.

Sadie leaned closer. "Jessie, this isn't your fault."

It wasn't my fault that he made that choice, but I wouldn't kid myself into believing in my innocence. I wanted to leave but wouldn't, because of the girls. I told him so.

I looked down at Oberon's black fur covering my feet. He followed me from room to room after Jake left.

"It hurt Jake to imagine that I'd only stay for the kids. To him, it's always been about the two of us. And that only played into the narrative that I had about him."

"What do you mean?" She got up to grab the teapot from the kitchen and refilled our cups.

"I think he's less inclined to sacrifice for their benefit. He wouldn't give up something important to him so the girls could have more, when the opposite feels natural to me. I'd give up a date night for a family night because that felt like the best thing for the girls, and he'd be upset because he wanted time alone with me. That made him seem selfish to me, so I took what I'd otherwise give to him, and give it to the girls on his behalf. Over time, to both of us, it became me and the girls on one side, and him on the other."

She sat back down next to me, putting her hand back on mine. "We talked all summer about how much you wanted to *stop* sacrificing things that were important to you."

It took me a long time to realize, in that respect, Jake may have been right all along. He loved spending time with the girls, but not to the exclusion of everything that made him who he was. We just started figuring it out but I guess the damage had already been done. He blew up all of our progress to tell me about something that happened a year ago.

Sadie frowned. "How long have things been bad?"

"I could tell you six months but if I went back two years, I could see it. I told myself I did what I had to do because I made a commitment and we were a family, but I didn't think about losing the person I love." I focused on Sadie's weathered, red leather shoes. "When things were bad, I thought about how much easier life would be without having to walk on eggshells—held hostage to his moods. I dreamed about the freedom to make my own decisions without considering him. Jesus, last winter when he left for a work trip, I fantasized about getting a call that his plane crashed and imagined myself free of the mess without having to accept any responsibility."

Sadie raised her eyebrows at me.

"I didn't actually want him to die; I wanted relief from the struggle. I stopped seeing him as anything but a problem."

I know that I'd given him the impression many, many times that I could live without him—that I wasn't there for him. When he got stressed and volatile, it triggered something inside of me and the walls came up. Last night, when I imagined someone else knowing him the way that I did, those invisible walls were nowhere to be found. I walked into our bedroom last night overwhelmed with love for this person who has walked beside me through the best and worst moments of my life. He cannot be replaced.

Sadie tilted her head, her warm eyes comforting me, and she asked how we left things.

"We need time. I couldn't believe that he agreed; in the past, he balked at the idea of time apart. He said he'll do whatever is necessary to save this." I peeked in the window at the girls then back at Sadie. "Right now, I know it wasn't about that woman—that *Tracy*. The issue is everything else that got him to that moment. I wish he never told me about her. We were doing so well, but he had to unburden his conscience."

"The secrets would color everything, Jess. The shame would've kept him from being the partner you deserve. Look at how that played out for Mia, and the way secrets held her back and held our relationship back. At least now you have a real chance to fix what got you to this point, if you want to." Sadie always knew what to say.

I smiled at her. "I'm glad you're here with me. I couldn't handle Mom today but I really needed someone."

Sadie said, "She'll be a mess because she doesn't know how to fix this. She woke up this morning so agitated. Why haven't you talked to us before this?"

"I thought that Jake and I were handling it. We *were* handling it." I took a deep breath. "And I suppose that part of me worried that she'd blame me."

"Jessie, no..." Just then the doorbell rang, interrupting Sadie. "It's probably Mia. She sensed that we've been talking about her."

I walked through the back door, peeking at the girls, then through the house to the front door to find Mrs. Carini and her granddaughter, Isabella, standing outside. I narrowed my eyes and leaned forward as my brain tried to place her. I couldn't imagine Mrs. Carini anywhere but in Presston, and certainly never at my front door.

45. MIA

Nana Wanda slammed the front door as she left. I tiptoed back to bed and fell asleep to the sound of Mama's tortured wailing after their fight. Later, the sound of her singing voice woke me up—ethereal in the back yard. I listened from my bed, feeling relieved and safe. Just as I started to fall back asleep, Mrs. Carini's voice startled me. She spoke harshly in Italian as I shuffled to my bedroom window.

In her housecoat, with rollers in her hair, Mrs. Carini stood over Mama pleading in Italian. Mama, in her underwear, laid on her side in the spot where she pulled flowers earlier that day. She continued singing, though more softly, cupping handfuls of soil and rubbing it into her arms—bathing in it. The soil clung to the skin of her arms in a reddish-brown paste. She paid no attention to Mrs. Carini, who turned in frustration toward our back door.

I heard her come in, calling for Daddy. He followed her out, stumbling down the cement stairs, and saw Mama. He looked afraid. He ran over to the shed and grabbed the old blanket that Mama folded up to kneel on when she worked outside. Mrs. Carini took it from him and wrapped it around Mama. Speaking softly, she sat down next to her on the ground and held her, wrapped in the blanket. Just then, Mama looked up and saw me in the window. A tear rolled down her cheek into the corner of her mouth.

That night, she laid on the very ground beneath me. We celebrated Jess's 32nd birthday with a picnic on that spot—Mama's age on the night she meant to end her life. I remembered her infectious joy at the pancake picnic, when she imagined what we could create with the empty canvas of our back yard. It started as grass, spots of rocky soil, and a chaotic field of weeds leading to woods. It became lilacs, peonies, and a fieldstone path to the woods bordered by goldenrod. It looked like the garden of someone with a peaceful spirit and an ordered soul.

After that night, Mama stayed in her room. She didn't want to see anyone. Nana Wanda told us that Mama wasn't feeling well and came by after daily mass every morning to get our breakfast. She made us cheese sandwiches with mayonnaise when we got home from school and sat with us while we played, crocheting a beautiful purple princess doll for me that I named Priscilla. She never told us about the baby.

"Mia Maria, what are you doing back here? You scare me to death." Mrs. Carini startled me out of my memories, in her purple caftan dress and heavy gold earrings.

I said nothing and reached into my pocket for a tissue to blow my nose.

She continued, "I look out the window and see your mother digging in the dirt. The way you sit and move your arms, just like Mama. Then you act crazy? Tearing up this beautiful garden?"

"Crazy?" I laughed. "Then I am just like Mama, aren't I?"

I told her that we both saw Mama out there bleeding into the ground that night—her *nervous breakdown*. Mrs. Carini calmly walked into Daddy's house and came back a minute later with a glass of water.

"Drink and calm down, for goodness sake. I'm too old for this excitement." She handed me the water and walked back toward the door, easing her creaking bones onto the steps of the stoop. "I haven't thought about that night in a long time. We let it die with your Mama." She folded her hands in her lap. "How did you see?"

"From my bedroom window." I pointed at the window above us. "I watched it all happen."

"That is so much truth for a little girl. So much that you still cry about this? An old woman yourself?" She took a deep breath and softened her voice. "You cannot know what it was like for us, Mia Maria."

Exhausted, I sat on the ground and sipped my water—bewildered by her gentleness.

She continued, "You think I wanted baby after baby? Always with a child at my breast? Church says baby is a gift from God. God says obey my husband." She seemed to struggle with her words for a moment, then continued. "It's what my mother did and her mother before her." She stared off toward the woods. "I had babies and lost babies, whether I wanted another baby or not. I had no one to help—not my husband, bless his soul." She looked up at the sky.

I recalled Jessie's struggles, even with help and support.

Mrs. Carini went on, "Your Mama was a different kind of woman—not practical, like me." She flicked her hands toward the woods. "She walked around in the dark and I didn't understand her, but she loved you girls. Anyone could see. Even if she couldn't be the Mama you wanted..."

"It didn't diminish her love?" I asked, knowing the answer.

"No, or her pain when she let you down. It's complicated, I know, but life is complicated, no?" She folded her hands, bringing them to her chest. "The night she had the nervous breakdown, she said, 'My girls, I love my girls. I buried my heart for the girls,' and I said she's out of her mind because of the blood."

She looked over at the garden. "You girls are what she thought about in her darkest hour. Your poor Papa didn't know how to help her, but he tried, more than most men would."

She reached up and took off her clip-on earrings, holding them in her cupped hands. "Your Papa was lost when she died, for a long time. Thank God for your Nonna. A holy woman." She made the sign of the cross.

She remembered talking with him on the porch after the evening news every night. "He checked on me, especially after Mr. Carini passed. I know you had trouble with your Papa. He talked about that." She put the earrings down next to her on the step and smoothed the front of her dress. "He said you blamed him. But what could he do except keep trying?"

I let my shoulders fall forward. It was easier for him to love Sadie; she accepted it so gratefully. He and I had a more complicated relationship. Like war buddies, we went through something together, but never discussed it.

Mrs. Carini said, "After that night, I tried to forget what I saw. I prayed for her. I prayed for you all. But seeing you out here tonight..."

Her voice slowly returned to the gruffness I was accustomed to. "From my kitchen window, I saw her before it happened." She reached out for my hand as she stood up. "She dug into the ground where the pink flowers grow, like a dog burying a bone. I thought maybe she might bury the metal box at her feet; she was strange like that. But then it all went bad." Mrs. Carini put her hand on my shoulder, lifting half of her expression into a smile and left me alone in the garden.

I imagined Mama lying on the ground telling Mrs. Carini that she loved us. It was an odd expression: *burying her heart for us.* Through my tears, I felt compelled to dig up the pink peonies. Sure enough, as I got closer to the bottom of the root ball, I hit metal. Confused, I dug deeper to reveal a small, rectangular, metal bank with a slot for coins on the top and a silver button on the side. I wiggled it out of the ground, brushed it off, and used my fingernails to pick out the dirt packed around the silver button on the outside so that I could press it in to open the box.

Inside, I found two rolled up papers with a bracelet around them like a napkin ring. The coppery bracelet snapped open in the middle to snap closed around your wrist. There were copper leaves and acorns, green from weathering, along the outside. It looked both unusual and familiar. I remembered it on Mama's wrist. I remembered how we gathered acorns in the woods and brought them back to the house. Mama decorated the mantle behind Daddy's chair with them. In the winter, she cut evergreen branches for the mantle so the living room smelled like the woods.

I brushed the dirt off of the bracelet and after some pulling, got it open. I put the bracelet on and felt Mama's presence immediately.

I remembered it on her wrist and the green dress that she used to wear with it. I smelled her perfume and felt her hand on my cheek, warm like the sun on my face the morning that we ate pancakes in the back yard. I heard her laughing with her friend Lillian, who seemed to have a fondness for it. It was the bracelet from the diary. I slowly unrolled the first sheet of paper and caught my breath at the sight of her handwriting.

My Dear Mia,
Your sister is too young, but you are an old soul, so I write for you and know that you will share what needs to be shared. I look into your eyes and I sense that you perceive what's happening. What mother burdens her children with the truth of who she really is? I started keeping diaries so that, one day, you might see who I really am...now I'm not sure I remember myself. I imagined for a time where I would bury my heart for you and I chose the pink peonies that you love. I don't know if you'll ever read this but I bury it for you anyway and in the process I feel peace. I imagine my heart cells breaking apart and joining the soil and the roots. I imagine you cutting the flowers and smelling them—that I might still touch your face, feel your hands, and watch you sleep from the bedside vase.

I think of the very first raspberry bush we planted together and the light that came out of you that day. You looked at me and saw a magical creature. While we planted, side by side, I remembered being young and connected to the earth and to spirits. I never felt alone.

I'm caught between two worlds now. Under the trees and in the soil, I'm at home in my skin. In the rest of my life, I'm defeated. It pains me to think that you've only had glimpses of me before this sadness infiltrated my body. It pains me to think that you'll only remember me the way that you see me now—the way that your Nana sees me.

My love may have looked different to you from that of other mothers but I assure you it is as fierce a love as I could produce. I think that I am too much for this world, dear one, but you...you are just enough. You and Sadie are all that is good in me and your

father and so much more. You bloom triumphantly, even in de-
pleted soil—my most beautiful contribution to this place.
With all of my love, my dearest one,
Mama

I unrolled the second sheet of paper. It appeared to be a kind
of poem ripped out from her diary. In her handwriting, I read:

It comes on slowly. I wake up with a poem stamped on my eyeballs
and the smell of lilacs in my nose. I'm living in my skin and the
bottoms of my feet kiss the ground as I walk. I drag my fingertips
over everything I pass. I need to feel. I want everyone to taste the
air that I taste. I gather Paul and the girls and feed them the air
and dance in the kitchen to Sarah Vaughn.

In my garden, I work furiously. When the moon is bright
enough, I stay out all night. I cross the border to the sacred, a con-
nection to something bigger than myself where moments are as
pure as sex and birth and death. Every walk among the trees in-
spires me and I leave the girls sleeping in their beds to find Paul
and make plans. I find his smiling eyes, familiar smell, and strong
arms. We stay awake together all night long remembering who
we used to be.

Sometimes I disappear to Lillian and her soft ankles and
long hair, braided to one side. I bring poems and we smoke cig-
arettes and listen to Billie Holiday sing about love that cannot
live until the sun comes up.

It comes on slowly. My eyelids are weighted by expectations
and it's better to sleep. I cannot remember Lillian or gather my
family. I cannot find the strength to form a thought or a word
for my husband. I have no smile for my young daughters. I'm of
no use and I must imagine myself a molecule in the soil, in the
flowers, in the air, in the moonlight to somehow breathe again.

I wait until the whole house is dark to crack open this hard
cocoon and feel my way downstairs and out into the air. I miss
my children. At night, in the quiet, I long to be their mother. The
nurturing that I can't find for them flows out into the garden.
Using the shears from inside of the shed, I cut flowers for each of

my daughters and bring them with a pitcher of water into their room, surprised each time that no one ever wakes when I come in. I leave the flowers in the small vases by their beds, spending time by each of them, memorizing my daughters and praying that they feel safe and loved.

As time went on, it became harder to mother my daughters in the light, so the black raspberry bush became ferns by the shed, roses by the gate, and pink peonies in the corner where I bury my heart.

I rolled the pages back up and overwhelmed by my own tears, put them back inside the metal box, keeping the bracelet on my wrist. A great gust of wind blew through the back yard and the scarlet branches of the red twig dogwood swayed in the distance.

46. JESS

" **J** es-see-ca, we need to talk."

She didn't greet me—no *sorry for dropping in unan-nounced.* Mrs. Carini pushed her way into my front door as soon as I opened it. She could be warm, but never friendly, and stood tall with large breasts and hips. As a child, I loved watching her hang her laundry outside, fascinated by the large brassieres swinging in the wind like colorful flags....beige, black, white, and one scandalous, faded red. Once her husband passed away, she told my mom that she had no energy for modesty.

I shrunk into my childhood body in her presence and nervously stepped aside. "Hello Mrs. Carini. Sadie's on the back porch. Come join us."

Isabella's expression begged forgiveness as she helped her grandmother through the hallway to the kitchen. Mrs. Carini's head moved from side to side taking in the bright colors with disdain and making a mental note of every spill, stain, and tumbleweed of dog hair that she passed. Through the window, I watched Sadie's horrified expression as she looked up from the back porch.

Mrs. Carini's voice sounded demanding no matter the message. "Sadie, I am worried. You girls are feral like your mother."

"Mrs. Carini, this is a surprise." Sadie answered, looking up at me for help.

The old woman held onto her granddaughter and stepped through the back door. "I worry. Word gets out about empty houses. Mrs. Buczynski's grandson gets his drug money from copper pipes in empty houses. Did you know that? I keep watch on the house, but I worry. Why don't you sell? You have enough problems."

Sadie's eyes scanned her surroundings for an escape path, but Mrs. Carini blocked the door. "That's Mia," she told her. "I want to sell. You need to talk to her."

"Talk to Mia? She is craziest of all. Earlier, I hear the metal clanging and jump up to the window, sure to see Mrs. Buczynski's grandson. I grabbed the phone and pulled the curtains aside and what do I see? Mia Maria ripping up plants—digging your mama's flowers up with the big shovel. She ripped out the whole garden. I said to myself, well she's lost her mind like her mother, rest her soul." She made the sign of the cross and shook her head. "God bless you; you're all mad. I come to see Jes-see-ca to find if *she* will see sense." She pointed a long, crooked finger at Sadie. "I want you to talk to your sister about selling the house to my Isabella. She will move there with her daughter and be close to me. I'm getting old."

Isabella smiled meekly from the corner of the porch, raising her eyebrows at the idea that her grandmother was just now getting old. "I'm on my own with my daughter now and it would be a good space for us," she said. "She'll have kids to play with and be near Nonna."

I rubbed my eyes trying to make sense of everything. "Ladies, thank you for coming by. You've given us a lot to think about, but right now, we need to check on my mom. We'll have to get back to you." I motioned for Isabella to get her grandmother out of there.

"I'll try to get her on the phone," I mouthed to Sadie, making a phone motion.

"Thank you, Mrs. Carini. Thank you, Isabella." I picked up the phone and started dialing before Mrs. Carini walked back inside the kitchen.

Mrs. Carini wrapped her long fingers around my wrist and lowered her voice. "Jes-see-ca. You need to go find your mama. She needs you girls."

Mom's phone line rang in my ear as I walked straight through to the front door waiting to escort them out. "Yes, thank you. We'll be in touch soon."

"Jes-see-ca, why is your home like a circus? So many colors. Where are little girls?"

"Thank you, Mrs. Carini. I'll bring them by soon." I closed the door right behind them, grateful the girls hadn't moved from their movie, and went back out to Sadie.

"She isn't answering," I said. "Will you stay here with the girls? I'll go over to the house and see what happened in the garden." I grabbed my keys on the counter by the diary, impulsively grabbing it too. "It doesn't make any sense."

She handed me my purse. "Of course. Call me from the house. I'll keep trying to get a hold of Mia."

I put the diary inside my purse and walked to my car, grateful to leave the house and drive in peace. The maple tree across from the Presston footbridge welcomed me to the neighborhood with a burst of red. When I turned off of the industrial road and drove down Ohio Street, I noticed children everywhere. Two girls rode pink bikes down the sidewalk to my left and a larger group of kids drew with chalk on the cement near the park. A boy and a girl swung side by side and kicked off their shoes at the same time. I pulled up to the house hoping to avoid Mrs. Carini and walked around the side to the back garden.

I slowly turned in a circle, taking it all in: bare patches where the ferns grew by the shed and an empty hole where the pink peonies once blossomed. I sat down on the bare ground at the edge of the garden where Mom spared the still-blooming goldenrod and leaned up against the shed. It didn't make any sense to me that she would show up here on her own. Destroying everything wasn't her way.

I called Sadie to fill her in.

"Mia's here with us," she said. "Everything's okay. We're having a tea party with Sarah and Amelia; it's exactly what she needs right now. Everything's going to be okay."

Relieved, I took my time gathering the plant debris my mom left behind. Even in the mess, it felt like the first real breathing that I'd done in the previous 24 hours. I had one more diary entry to read after a spot where a few pages were torn out. It seemed fitting to read it in the garden. I sat down with my back against the shed as the wind blew through, rustling the spent, tall grasses planted on the borders. Pink and beige plumes danced within the grasses and whispered an ambient, soothing sound as I retrieved the red book from my purse.

Dear Diary,   *October 24, 1964*

I spend all day sitting in this chair by my bedroom window, watching the serpentine pattern of cold rain pooling and sliding down the front walkway. These are the last of the rainy autumn days and soon it will be winter. I read once that the clean, biting cold of winter is the time for ghosts, even though most people would say the veil is thinnest now.

All of the women in my family have felt the pull of spirits. Maybe it's the Catholic upbringing, or maybe the legacy of strong women, forced to stand on their own and guided to trust the one thing that they could: their intuition.

The people that I've loved who passed from this world, did so in the quiet peace of a room that looked out at windswept, glittery, snow globe snow. My grandmother Teresa died the winter I turned ten years-old. I stood, amazed, at the cold, hard flesh in the casket, clutching a plastic cross. I waited there for hours during the viewing, watching for movement in her chest. The whole ritual felt sacred and full of secrets. In spite of her cruelty, before she died, my babcia sat in church every Sunday caressing her rosary. She fully expected to be welcomed into heaven, but even as a child, I wasn't so sure.

I have these fantasies about what my children will think of me when I'm dead and gone. I never feel like I communicate my love in a way that will last and overpower all of the times when I've lost myself and failed them. I take comfort in the fact that I still remember my babcia fondly, despite her malice. Now that I'm older, I understand the impact of her carelessness on Mumma, and me by extension, but she didn't leave any diaries to help us understand what made her so hard.

She cared for me when Mumma worked. In her house, I felt like a part of a family. She scared me, but I knew I belonged to her. I didn't always belong to Mumma, who usually seemed uncomfortable with me, unless we were at Babcia's. We both belonged there somehow, like sisters...strange.

My babcia got meaner as she got sicker, but I remember a very clear moment during her funeral that the fleeting glimpses of her loving kindness started coming back, one at a time. I remembered the way she put her arm around me when we listened to her favorite radio programs in the evening and the times she bought my favorite cookies at the bakery even though she didn't like them. I even remembered the few instances that she tried to right her wrongs—rare occurrences as she was never wrong and rarely sorry. It served as more proof of the magic of death.

I've never been afraid of death or leaving places unvisited and tasks unaccomplished. It's given me the freedom to take risks and a fearlessness that made me feel more alive.

The fear comes from being accountable to the people I love. DK

I closed the diary and took a minute to sit quietly in Deenie's garden. I got up and walked around to the other side of the house to turn the hose on and water the remaining plants. It felt like a kindness after what happened. Looking out toward the railroad tracks, I decided to take a walk toward the woods. I wasn't ready to go home.

The leaves of the old birch tree were a brilliant, golden yellow. The ghostly white bark reached up into the clear blue sky. It peeled open straight down the front like a book opening. I grabbed a hold of the lowest limb and walked my legs up the trunk. With some effort, I steadied myself and climbed higher into a nook made by the trunk and limbs that looked like an open palm.

From high up, I surveyed all of Presston. A family sat at a picnic table covered with food and talked across the chain link fence to the elderly couple next door. Two children ran out of their front door to greet their mother as she returned home. I rubbed my eyes and watched a little girl holding an old man's hand as they walked down the street toward the beer garden.

Tears filled my eyes and overflowed down the sides of my face. I missed Grandpa. It was such a gift to see myself through his eyes as I grew up. I missed that sense of validation and belonging. I think that's what Jake and I used to do—reflect our best selves back to each other. Somewhere along the way, it became the opposite.

I didn't want to look for myself in someone else's eyes. Sitting in that tree, I felt more like myself than I had in years.

47. MIA

The night that Mama died, Sadie and I slept at Nana Wanda's house. She answered the telephone that evening and I could hear Daddy screaming and wailing on the other end. She spoke calmly, hung up the phone, and put us to bed. The next morning, she told us at breakfast that something terribly sad happened. Our Mama got very sick and fell asleep and couldn't wake up. We never saw her again.

We lost her long before that day. I couldn't pinpoint when it started; she disappeared like day into dusk. We stayed alert for signs of darkness and clung to any shred of light she offered. She surprised us occasionally, slow dancing around the kitchen with Daddy to Sarah Vaughn and laughing her big laugh—the sound of hope. The next day, her vacant eyes or vacant chair across from me at the kitchen table felt like a little death—the promise of our happy family dying all over again. For so long, I hated Mama for all of those little deaths and the way they shaped me and shaped our family. I didn't think about what it must have been like for her to experience them. She looked into our eyes, knowing what was happening to us, but powerless to stop it. She didn't just try to stop her own pain but ours as well. She couldn't remember the ways that she made life magical for us, but she created and discovered beauty in places that no one else could. Then it came to me, as I sat in the remnants of her garden.

I wrapped my knit shawl around my shoulders and walked around the garden, the woods, and all throughout Presston. Walking down the alley between the two streets, I noticed all of the back yard gardens in the neighborhood for the first time. In several spots down the alley, I found a rainbow of chalk drawings. One particularly elaborate one said, *I will always love the moon and the stars* in a child's hand, with colorful stars and moons drawn horizontally across the alley.

I turned left and passed the old footbridge that Nana Wanda used to take us across for adventures. At the bottom of the metal steps, we picked mulberries. I rounded the corner to the beer garden and remembered standing outside as a child to listen to the laughter and music—an oasis in our town. *Tie a Yellow Ribbon* played in my head, and I teared up, remembering Daddy singing that song with Jessie and playing the harmonica part as she clapped along. I walked down Ohio Street toward the house, shielding my eyes from the sun, and got an idea.

It all began with the peonies. I split the pink peonies into three that day: one for me, one for Sadie, and one for Jessie. Every year, Mama's heart could bloom and watch over us. I imagined the cut blooms in my little pink vase, moved into my home after we cleared everything out of Daddy's. I stopped tending to Deenie's heart in the shadows of the past. For a long time, I'd been remembering, hearing, and talking to those shadows. Deenie's heart belonged out in the world and my heart belonged with the living. As the train rumbled past, I knew that the time had come—time to be brave and incandescent.

48. JESS

With the garden work finished, Mom instituted a new tradition for the fall and winter: a weekly Sunday brunch at her house. Over pumpkin French toast casserole and hot coffee, I listened to Mom and Sadie rediscover shared memories. At our first brunch, Sadie noticed that Mom wore the acorn bracelet that she told us about when she shared Deenie's last letters.

"An acorn has the potential to grow into a mighty oak, Mia," Sadie offered.

"Maybe this is the beginning of my mighty oak journey," Mom answered.

After brunch today, I put on my coat and walked outside to my grandmother tree. The sound of the wind through the dead, brown leaves hanging onto the oaks calmed my busy mind. Mom intended to plant an oak tree for Sarah and another for Amelia. She told the girls as they watched them grow, she would tell them about Deenie at her most magical. After that last day in the garden, there was a softness in my mom's expression and an ease in the way she carried herself that I'd never seen before. People fall apart, they seek help, and they recover. It happens all the time.

The scratchy, tap dance clicking of tiny feet beckoned my eyes upward as two squirrels chased each other up and around the black walnut tree. I spent the first few weeks after Jake left tunneling through our history. How did this happen? Could I have done anything? Questions about my fault in the matter became peace that no one was at fault, became we were both at fault, became everything was his fault.

Some days, it felt like I could walk away from him forever if we didn't have to see one another every week to give or receive our daughters. In the beginning, I arranged for him to pick them up from my mom's house. I couldn't face the prospect of him knocking on our front door like a guest. I talked to the collar of his shirt, terrified to meet his eyes. If he looked directly into my eyes for longer than a few seconds, I might start crying and never stop.

If our girls weren't there, I wouldn't have to pretend that I didn't hate him for blowing up our life to unburden his conscience. I resented smiling cordially—making small talk with the person I made children with. I begrudgingly told him about their new favorite snacks, wondering why he should have the privilege of understanding anything about me or our girls that he wasn't there to witness. Then a moment later, I'd close the door behind them and sink down onto the kitchen floor like a deflated balloon, wishing they'd turn around and come back home so we could all stand near the sink together making apple crisp.

After breakfast that morning, Sadie and I finished our coffee at the dining room table while Mom arranged dried, rose-tinted hydrangeas into a creamy white pitcher. She said that keeping the truth from Sadie crippled their relationship. I could only imagine what that might do to my marriage. It occurred to me that if I could forgive Jake, and myself, we could be closer the way that Mom and Sadie had become closer.

The idea of forgiveness was easier than the practice. Some days I had to hide how much I missed him. I wouldn't let him guess that I wanted him to come inside and pretend with me that nothing bad ever happened. I felt that way when he arrived yesterday as the girls packed toys upstairs with my mom to bring to his apartment.

He tilted his head, smiled, and grabbed my hand. "Will you come outside with me?"

I followed him to the front door, led by the hand. Outside, he walked down onto the sidewalk and leaned against the telephone pole by the strip of grass that I dug up to plant spring bulbs.

"I got a new job. It seems like a less stressful environment and the money's better. I don't want to pressure you, but I want you to know that I'm doing the work that I need to do. I want to be worthy of you and this family."

"It's not about *worth*," I interrupted.

He smiled. "While you take the space you need, I'll be doing the work that I need to do."

SPRING

49. JESS

The day before the first day of Spring, Sadie left a beautiful, brown leather journal embossed in gold foil roses at my back door. It had a red satin ribbon tied around it and a red rose tucked inside. She wrote *Rose medicine for forgiveness XOXO* on the inside cover.

She suggested I start journaling, to work through my *complex emotions*. She took turns with my mom all winter, watching the girls on Saturday mornings while Jake and I went to therapy and breakfast afterward to debrief. As the weeks went on, the breakfasts felt less like debriefs and more like dates. He said and did all the right things, but the sting of betrayal lingered. It took a few weeks, but eventually, I started writing.

Dear Jake,   April 11, 2010
On the day that Sarah tripped at the museum and hit her head on the edge of a marble column, by instinct, something in my body reached for you. I moved quickly to help her as reality settled in—I no longer had a partner behind me when life got scary. Our separation stopped hovering around my body and landed hard inside of it.

Someone brought me a handful of those cheap brown paper towels from the bathroom and I held them against the top of her head feeling the vivid colors of my anxiety grow and spread out like the bright red spot through the rough brown paper. Mom met us at the hospital and took Amelia home, leaving me alone with Sarah. I couldn't pretend to be brave for her then fall apart in your arms later. I couldn't meet your eyes in the room and share the fear without her seeing. I smiled and told her everything would be better soon and held my breath until my body forced an exhale.

Afterward, I carried her, freshly stitched, down the long hallway that bridged the hospital and the parking garage. Both sides were enclosed in glass—a mini museum that we passed when I was in labor a few hours before we welcomed her into the world. You marveled at the antique medical instruments. I pointed out the paintings of the Sisters of Mercy who established it as the first hospital in Pittsburgh in the 1800s. Even through the pain of back labor, I watched our reflection in the glass—distinctly aware that our life was only just beginning.

In the delivery room, you lovingly pushed your fist into that one spot in my lower back every time the lines on the monitor began their ascent. Our baby girl was determined to be born face up. You held her all night long while I slept and I woke several times to the moonlight reflecting off the wetness in your eyes.

Being back in that hallway without you, I ached for the feeling of a new beginning and hoped that we were somewhere in the middle and not at the end. Your face was lined with shame the first time you knocked on our front door to pick up the girls. As the weeks went by, your energy evolved until I wasn't sure which version of you to expect. Some days I opened the door to an imaginary wall so thick that you were blurry in front of my eyes. Some days an intimidating presence announced your arrival as you rounded the corner, but more often, the old defeated emptiness and stench of regret.

You had the audacity to arrive looking unaffected once, after I spent the better part of the day mired in my own feelings of betrayal. One morning, like remembering a dream, it occurred to me that I didn't need you to keep acknowledging my pain. My healing was entirely in my hands. The more we healed, the more

I recognized shades of who we used to be and the way we used to love each other. I noticed a hint of wonder in your eyes when you leaned over to pick up Amelia, and eventually even hope when we met at the front door. You laid yourself bare before me, took responsibility, asked for forgiveness, and made it safe for me to do the same. Quietly, gently, and with the utmost care, we started to find each other again.

I imagined that a deep love should slowly flicker and pop and fizzle and gasp until its last breath. Something as carefully woven together as two lives, wrapped up and around each other, would have to be slowly unwound and knots untied, with the same kind of care that went into the weaving. Like the yarn in our kitchen that Sarah draped and wound from knob to knob in a zigzag pattern, some may have to get scissors and cut straight through to pull it apart, but we had the space to unwind it.

It's my greatest hope that we can reweave it into something stronger and more colorful than it ever was.

Yours,

Jess

One Saturday, after therapy and breakfast, we picked up the girls together and came back home, passing the jewel-toned purple crocuses emerging near the telephone pole by our front stoop. The girls chased the dog through the back door to play in the yard and I shared that letter with Jake as a token of my commitment. He stood near the kitchen window and read it, put the journal down on the butcher block, and pulled me close. We were almost there. We both felt it.

It took some time for me to realize that the last barrier to that goal was finding a way to forgive myself. In our kitchen, he put his index finger on my lips when I tried to take responsibility for my part.

He shook his head. "We've said it all. Don't you think?"

I held both of his hands. "I need to say the words and for you to receive them." He knew from the look on my face to let me speak. "I'm sorry for the times when you felt discouraged and my response made you feel unsupported," I said. "There are so many things I would do differently. Our marriage is precious to me, and I cherish you and the life we built together. I need you to know that going forward."

Jake smiled through tears and wrapped his arms around me. I closed my eyes and leaned toward him and the sun streaming through our kitchen window. There was so much work into getting to that moment and more to do, but we persevered through the worst of it. Still in Jake's arms, I scanned the refrigerator and took stock of the minutiae of our little life hung on the front with magnets: the photo of us when we were younger, the pictures our children drew, the poems and fortunes that were special enough to keep and read over and over again. We rebuilt something sacred into something even more sacred. It was the hardest thing I'd ever done and just like the fortune cookie said: I emerged victorious.

50. DEENIE

Let me tell you a story from the depth of Mia's grief, the most tender spot of Sadie's mind, and the ache in Jessie's chest. My girls are healers. They heal Teresa's wounds, Wanda's wounds, and mine, along with their own. They liberate themselves from unhealed pain embedded in their bones. They refine our best efforts: Teresa's perseverance, Wanda's protection, and my imagination and wonder. They offer it, restored with new clarity, to their nieces and daughters to carry forward.

It's a privilege to watch them spin their lives into something more significant at every age. Sadie transmitted resilience and embodied compassion as she learned to plant roots deeper into the soil. Mia Maria gathered what the women before her left behind and fed it to the earth, scattering the remnants of her own pain in as well, to decompose. She cultivated new life there, slowly emerging with energy and color. Jess harvested it all and fed everyone rainbows. She wasn't afraid to be accountable to the people she loved.

51. JESS

I drove alongside the river toward Presston with the Pittsburgh skyline in my rearview mirror. It was one of those days when spring surrendered to summer and the air smelled different. Early June clarified muddled, fragrant spring into glossy, green leaves and fresh grass—warm wind without a chill chasing the tail end. The breeze blowing through the open car windows rearranged my hair in an easy, tender way, like a mother comforting her child. A deep inhale of that air made you feel things were possible, but it wasn't enough to soothe my unsettled heart.

The hours before a goodbye are more painful than saying goodbye. It felt heavy in my gut and hip bones, like the day I drove on that road to the funeral home in The Bottoms. When Grandpa died, I watched the city disappear behind me through cold, heavy droplets on a gray afternoon. I parked in the lot and sipped coffee in my car, waiting until the last moment to go inside. Everyone in Presston used the same funeral home with the dim, sickly, yellow lighting and Las Vegas wedding chapel interior—where the thick stench of lilies greeted you at the threshold and the casket would be in sudden, startling view as soon as you crossed it.

I threw the paper cup away outside and walked in, closing my coat around my exposed neckline. If your other senses betrayed you, the temperature inside the funeral home left little doubt as to what we were doing there—preserving the dead. I charted a course through the bodies standing in groups of four or five, disappearing into the white noise of their quiet conversations as I passed. With my eyes on the casket, the faces around me blurred into shapes and colors: ovals of white and dark hair, bows of magenta lipstick, rectangles of navy blue suit jackets. Overwhelmed by the mingling scents of hairspray, cologne, and funeral lilies, I held my breath and found a path to the sterile shell of the first important man in my life. Beneath the powder and waxy covering, I saw his warm brown skin and strong nose. I imagined his mischievous smile and heard his heavy, hearty laughter. I stared through his suit coat sleeves and imagined his strong, sun-bronzed arms—solid from years of twisting metal.

A year and a half later, on my way to stand in Deenie's garden one last time, I drove past the funeral home where I said goodbye to Grandpa. I continued on to Presston and turned down Ohio Street, driving slowly to take it all in. Mom and Sadie were both there when I arrived, tidying up a few things before Isabella moved in later that day.

"It feels like I'm walking into a funeral," I said, kissing them both.

"It's a hail and farewell. Deenie's garden has moved on," Sadie answered.

My mom didn't destroy the garden that day. She brought the magic out into the world. She got permission to create a garden at the far end of Presston park, transplanting Deenie's yellow peonies and orange daylilies. She planted roses and spring bulbs with a meandering path that led to a heavy wooden bench. She and Isabella applied for a grant to plant trees along the park side of Ohio Street.

"This is hallowed ground," I said. "But it isn't where she died, it's where she lived."

Sadie announced that she brought a poem for our final goodbye. "*Ode to a Woman Gardening* by Pablo Neruda." She said, "Everything grew from Deenie."

Sitting in the garden, I felt a wave of gratitude for the women who came before me. We all found ways to rebuild something sacred into something even more sacred. My mother Mia's identity was woven completely into the fabric of her relationships. Watching her release control and embrace her life with hope and surrender helped me to navigate motherhood in a brand new way.

Sadie—who Deenie might have been with the same support, prioritized her own care and her creativity and compassion overflowed in the most surprising ways.

And my grandmother, Deenie—I prayed that she watched over us from another dimension, as we spread beauty in our own ways and lovingly tended what fed her in her darkest days, with gratitude for her sacrifices. More than anything, I hoped that she felt proud of her true legacy: complicated women, strong women, magical women—women who loved themselves and each other and did the best they could.

After one last look around, we made our way to our cars. Mom hugged us goodbye and held on for a long time.

She let go and said, "I'll send you a postcard."

"Where are *you* going?" Sadie asked.

"I haven't decided. I'm just going to drive west and see where I end up."

Mom typically planned trips a year in advance. Sadie asked for details and Mom said there were no details to give. She finished the school year and had two months of freedom ahead of her with no responsibilities. She decided to take off and see where the road took her.

"I'll stay in touch. Don't worry," she reassured us, opening her car door.

"Drive all the way to the coast and get those toes in the sand!" Sadie called after the door slammed shut. Mom rolled her window down to wave.

I retrieved my voice. "You honestly have no plan? Mom, really, what is the plan?"

She turned toward me with wet eyes. "Maybe an upturned bowl of stars or a strawberry moon? Maybe Tucson."

I smiled, remembering Deenie's honeymoon trip, and waved goodbye. She started the car, blew us a kiss through the window, and pulled away as her gold St. Christopher medal swung from its chain around her rearview mirror.

This book is dedicated to the women who came before me—four generations of women who made a life for themselves and their children, often on their own. I have so much gratitude for their sacrifices and their courage—most especially for that of my mom, Chris Vitale.

Thank you to my fellow Wayward Writers and especially to my mentor and editor Ariel Gore. I've learned so much from you all. Thank you to my dearest friends Beth and Lisa for your hearts, your ideas, and your energy through this process. Thank you to my daughter Emma for her insight and encouragement, and to my kids Aubrey and Benjy for their support. Thank you to my love, Josh. There aren't enough words to describe how important you were in this journey. This story was written by all of us.

Amanda Gilby's grandparents and great grandparents lived and worked in Presston. Her work can be found in *Hip Mama,* the Literary Kitchen zine *Magical Writing,* and the anthology PLACES LIKE HOME. She can be found on instagram @amanda_gilby and in Pittsburgh—on her porch with a book or out front in the dirt. This is her first novel.